FORGOTTEN ROAD

Also by SIMON HARVESTER

Simon Harvester

FORGOTTEN ROAD

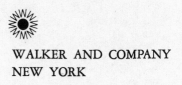

WALKER AND COMPANY
NEW YORK

First published in the United States of America
in 1974 by the Walker Publishing Company, Inc.

ISBN: 0-8027-5299-3

Library of Congress Catalog Card Number: 73-93934

Printed in the United States of America.

10 9 8 7 6 5 4 3 2 1

For James Macleod

My Dear James:
You have been foolish enough to take your eyes off the beauties
of Stornoway and the Isle of Lewis, Scarp and Taransay,
the curlews and herons and oyster-catchers, and the Hebrides, to
accompany me on several 'Roads'. Now this really is flattery!
With all that beauty beyond any door you open . . .
Such friendship deserves acknowledgement, however slight.
Indeed, if you need help to repel the foreign housebuyers, sound
your pipes and I'll arrive to man the barricades with you.
Meanwhile, for you and yours, a story to indicate gratitude for
good friendship.

Affectionately,

Simon

'It is useless for the sheep to pass resolutions in favour of vegetarianism while the wolf remains of a different opinion.'

Dean Inge

I

Silk glanced up as the helicopter clattered overhead like a dragonfly uncertain whether it should go down for a closer peer at him and his companions.

He had to narrow his eyes to slits to glimpse its outline clearly against the blazing blue sky. Now as earlier, unless he had been misled by its unfamiliar green and dust coloured paintwork, the distinctive toothpick tubular tail and the front composed almost entirely of perspex to give its pilot the maximum vision possible meant it was a German BO 105. He had seen one at a European air-show a couple of years or so ago and said he liked its appearance, whereupon Fathiya offered to buy him one for a non-birthday present; she often tried to do things like that. Its appearance here was unexpected. No markings identified it as belonging to the Pakistan Air Force.

Yet for the past half hour or so its two heavily goggled occupants had shown a policely curiosity in him and his companions, their machine whirling and rattling through the brilliant sunlight illuminating the bleak moutain-ringed valley as they walked along its barely used track among boulders, great spills of talus and scree, and occasional thickly-leafed glades whose shade remained hot and airless.

Heat and dust, a deepening sense of isolation, had become constant factors ever since they got off the bus to begin what should be the last if most unpredictable stage of their journey.

Silk glanced back. Each of the three porters they had hired

in Chitral to help with equipment essential in this region devoid of *daks* or other forms of shelter for travellers was watching the helicopter curiously. They had the lean hardness of mountain Pakistanis who scratched a living from whatever casual work came their way. Until the helicopter appeared they were more lively than when they climbed into the ancient but gaudily decorated bus at Chitral. Now, again, they were silent, foreheads lined, cheeks sunken under the habitual black stubble, eyes full of brooding unease.

Silk wished they could have brought Heron Murmur along instead of leaving him in Chitral. Murmur had a truly expert knowledge of hill-country porters all the way from Sikkim and the lower regions of Tibet, a knowledge born of years, and knew how to persuade them to talk readily about things which their inbred secretiveness kept hidden from strangers. But events had necessitated that he should be the one to remain behind.

As Silk looked up the valley to where its floor became a ridge and should dip steeply farther on, the helicopter hovered over a small wood several hundred yards ahead like a bee studying a clump of flowers. Its occupants were unquestionably curious about his party. Echoes of the helicopter engine, flung back from the steep hillsides, nearly deafened him. He wondered if the pilot was one of the modern innocents, brother to the motorist who had a jalopy with a new number-plate and which had to be taken for its drives and put through its tricks whenever he had an hour off.

Abruptly the helicopter lifted itself a couple of hundred feet into the air. It stopped, as if its occupants wanted to confirm details about Silk and his party, then swung about and clattered away down the valley. After some minutes the gnat-whine of its engine faded from their ears.

The afternoon returned to a silence interrupted only by the ceaseless pianissimo ecstacy of millions of flies queueing up in frenzied delight to gain the exotic nectar of human sweat. In the last few hours hundreds had indulged themselves to the point of intoxication. Silk heard the porters resume their whispered conversation. Its terseness betrayed distinct uneasiness.

'What d'you suppose that thing was after?' Wallace queried. Silk shook his head. 'I've no idea,' he answered. 'Probably they didn't expect to see us.'

He had not worked with Wallace for several years. Much to his regret, he had become a general dogsbody, too often separated from the lands and peoples of the Middle East which he knew and loved best of all despite present hazards. Angus Wallace was different. Unlike most erroneously labelled experts on political affairs in the Indian sub-continent, he had proved his knowledge and ability by accurate forecasts of events in division-riddled Pakistan. He spoke most local languages fluently: Urdu and the Afghan Pushtu, Hindi and Kashmiri, Tamil and Gujarati and Konkani among the many tongues of India. Up here among the grim hills of what was once known as the North-West Frontier, the region of the hardy Pathans among others, he had a working acquaintance with dialects of most Kafir valley tribes, even Khowar and the almost extinct Domali language. Silk knew none of these dying forms of speech.

Wallace was something over forty. As a young man he had studied law but abandoned it in favour of dealing in antiques. Twelve years ago a combination of itching feet and business acumen and a desire to see something of the world before it descended to the tourist level of hot dogs and fish-and-chips in plastic containers brought him to Pakistan. He was a large man, close on six feet tall, muscular, and light on his feet. His sleek black hair rioted over his head and his brown eyes were mild. He was popular, voluble on occasion, had brief flashes of temper, enjoyed large meals and played polo. He collected old Asian weapons which he patiently restored to approximately their original splendour of jewel-studded design in silver or gold adornment.

Silk had been elsewhere when, a few years ago, Wallace had abandoned his determination not to marry. His wife, the European-educated daughter of an Iranian dealer in rare books and ancient illustrations, was more than ten years younger than himself, a graceful little woman with a natural ability as an artist. Their childless marriage, begun in the colourful and noisy bustle of Karachi and now based on the somewhat quieter and less dusty city of Rawalpindi, gave every appearance of success. Silk never took such signs as proof.

'I don't remember Bell notifying us of a landing-field near here,' he commented.

Wallace nodded. 'No,' he agreed.

'Correct me . . . my memory is that the nearest are at Chitral and Peshawar on this side of the frontier, and Kabal over in Afghanistan.'

'Right.'

'Though I suppose there may be small fields near the camps where the military keep their Indian war prisoners. For a quick search if any of the prisoners escaped and tried to get into Afghanistan.'

'I think there may be four or five.'

'Mmmm. I wonder where it came from.'

'One of those?'

'The Afghans are too careful to have a pick-up run for Indian refugees.'

'Why should they, or anyone, risk another international clash now when they're doing better?'

'You have a point there,' Silk agreed. 'Are the camps still operating?'

'Only the government and top brass know the present situation.'

'I suppose a Pakistani taxi would have official markings.'

'They play it cagey sometimes. Like most others hereabouts.'

'Well, we may find out,' Silk said, and looked round at the hills. They had a brooding, mysterious, heavy sort of atmosphere. Beyond some he could just make out the snow-streaked caps of mountains. He had an unwelcome conviction and that if he had to live here or had undertaken their mission alone these hills would have his latent claustrophobia chattering at him like a drunken parrot.

Abruptly Wallace said: 'Something is wrong.' He kept his voice down to prevent being overheard by the porters.

'I thought you were more silent than usual. What is it?'

'I don't know. My bones have an instinct. It began several miles back, before that chopper appeared. I think there may be people up in the hills.'

'Watching us?'

'Yes.'

Silk slitted his eyes and glanced round again. He thought the theory a very real possibility though this golden afternoon patina of sunlight on their bleak brown-pink-ochre folds, the tiny grey or violet dimple shadows which told of caves or ledges, made it impossible to see where dusty-robed Pathans or any others might perch, singly or in clusters, to use the latest rifles being smuggled into the country from almost every side. Up here only the woods provided concealment in their shade, but these hills could hide armies now as they had in earlier times. Their formation had scarcely changed.

It needed scant imagination to take it from there. In most parts up here every stranger was unwelcome and in these valleys the Pakistanis had problems over making friends. Consequently few travellers were given what traditionally-minded Pakistanis called *melmastia*, hospitality. If rumour were true ever fewer were offered *nanawatai*, shelter and care for fugitives and including hospitality. For centuries the tiny inbred family clans which inhabited these valleys, amalgams of long-dead Aryan and Persian and Greek people who had come here and brought their religious practices, had fought violently to preserve their customs and privacy. Now, one after another, they were leaving the valleys and their way of life was dying out.

Silk wondered if there could be a connexion there with the reason for his visit here. It might well be, even though the valley clansmen were of little importance to the main argument in progress.

He opened his mouth to ask Wallace questions and shut it again. He had asked enough now. It was time to think for himself.

The main pattern was well known. Ever since the army's defeat in East Pakistan and that area's re-emergence as Bangladesh the western section of the country had been an area of separatist conspiracy and intrigue with the odd murder and kidnapping here and there to keep ordinary people fearful. Both, up here in the North-West Frontier Province and down south in the narrow belt under Afghanistan and reaching Iran, were directly attributable to the National Awami Party and the Azad Baluchistan Party. There were also bitter provincial disputes with the government Pakistan People's Party.

He fished out a handkerchief and wiped his sweaty neck. So? So, many Pathans, independent, proud as Lucifer of their connexions with the Pathans of Afghanistan, wanted to create a new state, Pushtunistan, which would reach from the Afghan frontier to the long curving bank of the Indus and bisect Pakistan down its entire length; if that happened, as the people who seized power in Afghanistan two months ago under Russian military direction intended it to happen, the Afghans would try to control all southern Pakistan including Sind and Karachi. Such a plan had been formulated when the British Labour government announced its intention, directly after World War Two, to quit India. The theoretical Pushtunistan was then called Pakhtunistan, intended to include areas inhabited by Pathans, Baluchis, Chitralis like the porters muttering behind Wallace and himself.

Ever since those days this frontier region had boiled or

simmered with politico-sectarian hatreds and family feuds. There were also vicious disputes within each group as to the amount of violence to be used. At places along the frontier life had many hectic hours.

In this dusty turmoil the small isolated valley communities of Black Kafirs were largely ignored by the partisans and secessionists and raiding gangs which surrounded them. Fifteen, even ten, years ago several valleys had such clans. Since then their numbers had dwindled steadily. Those who remained were left to die off. This was probably due to Pakistanis being Muslims and Kafirs being outside Islam; 'Kafir' was an Arabic word for 'unbeliever'. Some Pakistanis expected the Black Kafirs here to expire quietly if left alone, a less dramatic end than that of the Red Kafirs of Afghanistan. In eighteen-ninety-five the Afghans smashed and defiled Red Kafir religious houses and idols and sacred places, forbade their customs, and forced them to become Muslims, sending the men to work on the road and taking the comelier women into their households as concubines. Elsewhere such things still happened.

That was the broad political background to the information given to Silk when he undertook this mission.

He had kept it in the forefront of his mind as a factor for explaining what might have gone wrong. They would not know until they reached their destination. But it could give a clue.

As they reached the ridge in the valley floor Silk saw that the ground beyond sloped sharply down for about half a mile and then levelled out for perhaps two or three miles until it contracted into a narrow pass between two sheer hillsides which resembled a split caused long ago by one of the earthquakes still common to the region. Between this ridge and the distant pass a line of trees thinned and widened into a copse of wood and thinned and widened again. Scattered about were patches of pale yellowish grass similar to untidy tufts of hair.

15

Several hundred yards up the left-hand hillside a few scrawny wild goats searched for fodder.

At Wallace's suggestion they had a rest in the first copse. Although the thick foliage took sunlight off their heads the shade gave no cooler air. Silk could feel it up tight against his nostrils, short on oxygen. He looked at the trees.

'What varieties are these?' he asked. 'I know a monkey puzzle, and the difference between conifers and deciduous types, but that's my limit.'

'Don't ask me.' Wallace was wiping his face with a magnificent yellow handkerchief untastefuly decorated with huge crimson and blue flowers. 'I've no idea. Something has to go.'

'Point taken. When did you last come here?'

'Years ago, soon after I came to Pakistan.'

'No reason to visit the area.'

'None. Bell kept in touch regularly by radio and came down about three times a year for supplies, sometimes more often. He'd lost the taste for big city life. He was happy painting up here.'

'We don't all share your passionate attachment to cities.'

'One man's food...' Wallace said and stood up. 'We'd better get on.'

As they resumed their walk, Silk's thoughts reverted to what had occupied his mind when the chopper first clattered into sight. He seemed doomed to spend part of his trudging 'in the footsteps of Alexander the Great'. His published views on this peripatetic warrior had caused him trouble.

'Why the bright smile?' Wallace asked.

'Well...' Silk began. A few years ago he had wandered through an area of Afghanistan where the Macedonian adventurer had either become bored with his seemingly homosexual friend Hephaestion or had regained enough energy from an excursion across the Oxus when he slaughtered every man, woman, and child in one village, to think a spot of female temperament might enliven a man of destiny. So Alex had his draughty tent pitched up a damp hillside in order to be alone with a local Bactrian *bint*, and she overcame him with her beauty as she capered about in gauze and the family pearls. The event provided an early example of male avoidance of responsibility by hiding behind a woman's see-through slacks.

The *bint* had something. Her name, Roxane, clearly foresaw the age of celluloid epics unreeling in movie-theatres. She was said to have been a princess. Every *bint* who overwhelmed a brave warrior and turned him to jelly was bound to be a princess even if her Daddy had only two blind camels; it provided a gracious label for romantics. Alex made her socially respectable by taking her into the fold of his wives, all given the nice gloss of sacrifices to statesmanship, but it caused her to become what a distinguished American professor, Will Durant, called 'a negligible impediment'. And so indeed it proved.

Wallace was laughing. 'I should have read ancient history,' he said. 'But it always seemed too ancient.'

'Only yesterday.'

'Did he get away with it?'

'Oh, Alex had his good points. He was generous to his friends.'

'And he came up here?'

'He certainly did.'

Somewhere here the Greek legion and its camp-followers of women from a dozen countries pitched tents in a thickly wooded valley and lit fires to warm a chilly night. Sparks from one fire set alight to the local cemetery where the dead lay in open cedarwood coffins on the ground. What remained after wild dogs and birds of prey had eaten their fill burned fiercely and the light revealed a well-built stronghold on adjoining hills which wily local people told Alex was called

Nysa. Alex and his generals gazed on it with awe and excitement. Nysa! One reason for their Great Adventure. Nysa! The fabulous city! The shrine! Alex forgot his recent confrontation at the city of Massaga with the beautiful Indian queen of the Assacenians which persuaded him to let her too overwhelm him for reasons fully comprehended by her tactful husband—everyone hailed the bouncing male issue of diplomacy as a splendid method of ignoring racial prejudice—which was small beer to this firelit vision of Nysa. Here, these hardy warriors believed, came the original Mr Unisex, their own favourite god Dionysus on his fabled caper into Asia at the head of an army of drunken centaurs, cloven-hoofed Pans, satyrs, and revelling fairies. Dionysus: born a ferility goddess, transformed into a god of intoxication, ultimately a divine human sacrificed to save mankind. Dionysus: in whose memory virgin girls and energetic matrons back home in Greece had taken to the spring-clad hills to celebrate his resurrection by getting drunk and dancing and eating roots which put them in a state of *ecstasis*, drinking the blood and eating the flesh of a sacrificed bull which put them into a state of enthusiasm, *entheos*, meaning 'a god within' or possession by a divine spirit.

'As you said, only yesterday,' Wallace commented. 'The first drop-outs.'

'In Europe, according to present belief.'

'Would I be correct in assuming the women claimed any child they bore came from Dionysus?'

'Right.'

'What happened at Nysa?'

When dawn came Alex ordered his troops to spare the city. They held religious services, banquets, made sacrifices to Dionysus. Then, vindicated and radiant, Alex and his men climbed from Nysa to the wooded green slopes of Meros. There they found vegetation identical with what grew on their own mountains at home. A state of *enthousiasmos* united them. They

18

fashioned themselves garlands and chaplets of leaves and vines. They dashed about the woods possesssed by the dementia called 'the Dionysiac frenzy'. They chanted hymns, praised their god for having led them to this shrine, ensured that local women took full advantage of their divine opportunity to remember the visitation with pride. The revels lasted several days. Then Alex led his men and their followers off on the long journey down beside the Indus and across present-day Baluchistan on their march home.

'Where were the women's husbands?' Wallace asked.

'They're not mentioned.   Absent on urgent business.'

'And this happened when?'

'If my memory is correct in three-twentyfive B.C.'

'Now we're here, nearly three thousand years later.'

'A blink of God's eye,' Silk commented and looked down the valley. He forgot Alexander. 'Our inquisitive friend is back.'

Wallace looked up.

At the far end of the valley a faint drone had recommenced as the helicopter came in sight. Silk imagined differences. At first sight the gnat appeared to be flying lower than earlier, only a few hundred feet above the ground. It was flying faster and appeared to be heading straight for them. After only a few seconds the prudent coward inside him began to natter fearfully; it had a very sensitive nose for trouble. As the chopper increased speed and dipped lower he glanced round.

The immediate landscape caused his inner safety-first addicts to get quite tremulous. They were about midway between two copses with no near tree to provide genuine cover. A scatter of boulders would give partial shelter against an enemy on foot, but were as useful as hundreds and thousands on a birthday cake against one who could hover overhead. His internal coward's teeth jangled like an arpeggio on a dulcimer.

He saw that Wallace had shaded his eyes to watch the

chopper. Behind them the porters had stopped. They were silent.

'Any ideas?' Wallace asked in a flat tone.

'These boulders may help until we can run for the trees.'

They yelled at the men to shelter behind the rocks and ran towards two boulders ahead. A trail of small dust clouds fountained up towards them on their right side. The chopper wobbled like a dragonfly about to settle. Abruptly the twining noises of clattering engine and harsh chattery firing grated into the sunlight and battered the senses.

One of the porters shrieked. As Silk glanced back his left foot tangled with an unseen root or matted grass. He tried to keep his balance but fell full-length, unable to think fast enough to break his fall. His body thudded heavily on the ground, knocking air from his lungs. At the same instant something hit him a vicious blow. He cried out as a lurid scarlet blur streaked with black washed over his sight. Then the blackness spread out like a great lake of pain and he fell into it.

2

Beyond pain was quietness. At first the pain was too continuous for him to know that instinct told him it was there. In fragmented seconds of lucidity he supposed that the times when pain left him were when he slid back into unconsciousness. It did not seem to matter.

Once he managed to hang onto a strand of awareness long enough to shove himself up to his knees. Almost at once pain sawed viciously through his head. He fell into nothingness again.

At some instant a fear which he associated with instinct warned him that he must be ready to face danger. That made him angry and anger hurt his head. If instinct knew so much it could tell him what to do. He thought about that. It hurt him to think but he forced himself to do it. After a while he moved his fingers and toes slightly to see if he could control them and if the movement betrayed him to an enemy. They moved but nothing else happened. He longed to groan but kept silent lest the sound give him away. It surprised him to find he was lying on his stomach, the ground hot and scratchy against his face, his hands beneath his body. Each limb responded to his bidding but the effort to think hurt his head like red-hot swords going through his brain.

After some moments he opened his eyes and shut them against the instant torture of light. Light! He thought about it.

The effort to think seemed to go round corners and slide over rocks to save his head from a heavy insistent pulse of every form of pain. Nothing happened when he shifted his limbs more positively. That meant nothing. His enemies might be keeping still in order to fool him. He let his body go slack to renew its energy.

More than anything he wanted to sleep but knew he dare not.

Time passed before he turned over onto his back. How long he could not tell. His mind was too confused to know anything clearly, each action caused by some instinct or other which he obeyed directly he could endure the mental effort required. There was another long interval. Finally he managed to sit up. Still nothing happened. Not outside him. Inside was different. Everything sagged and swirled, bucketed and sprang, in a red and black vileness.

He braced himself and let his enemy head hang forward on his neck and somehow managed to endure. Gradually he drew up his legs and let his forehead rest on his knees. Neither helped much. Panic began to chew at the pain like malicious teeth.

He felt hot and confused. Burningly hot, insanely confused. Too confused to think. Out of some knowledge he had forgotten he knew he was concussed.

He waited until he had some confidence in himself and then dragged up his eyelids and shut them again and opened them more cautiously and lowered them to look around him. It did not help much to be seeing them through a reddish fog which cleared only gradually.

He managed to make out small clumps of unfamiliar trees in two directions. Between them, scattered around him, were large smooth old boulders like badly-shaped eggs. He was sitting on a thin gritty pathway between two steeply rising hillsides, a valley which rose above the trees at one end and whose other end he could not see. One hillside was almost covered by pale shadow, the other bright with the thick curdled sunlight you saw only in the late afternoon. He forced himself to go on looking, to forget sickness in his stomach. Above the sunlit hillside he could just see the glaring white snowcaps of mountain peaks far away. Alarmed, he shifted round on his backside, obeying a need to know. The movement caused the sickness to rise in his throat, sour and burning.

A thirst tormented his mouth.

He narrowed his eyes.

Some yards away a man lay on his back with arms and legs stretched wide.

It needed a considerable effort but ultimately he managed to reach the man by crawling on his hands and knees. He looked down into the man's face. The man was dead, his sightless eyes untroubled by the glaring blue sky. A stream of dried blood from the man's chest darkened his twill shirt, spread from beneath his body, and stained his dusty trousers. The skin stretched thin over the bones of the man's narrow face and bony hands was deep brown. The face had a dark stubble of several days old and the hair under a strange porridge-coloured cap had an oily-blue blackness. The open mouth had stiffened in a last rictus of pain. Across the tongue crawled insects, ants like those on the glazed eyes and blood.

He knelt beside the body for some time, trying to remember. The man was a total stranger. Or was that wrong?

Finally he scrambled to his feet. Immediately he fell full-length, unable to keep his balance. The same thing happened a second time. At the third attempt he stayed up though only just, swaying and full of nausea, the landscape bucketing and threatening to dissolve again. He lunged over to the nearest boulder and propped himself against it, breathing heavily. After a pause he gained courage. He turned his head slowly, regardless of the pain in it, looking around him. Everything was quiet.

Two other men lay farther off. He could tell from here they

were both dead though he knew he would have to be sure. Someone had set fire to things and pushed a boulder onto tins of what might hold food. There were several smashed water-bottles.

When he felt strength in his legs he got off the boulder and staggered over to the other two bodies. The men were dead. They had the same dark skin.

He went to a boulder and propped himself against it, trying to think. No sound reached him. Not even a whisper of air. He was completely alone. It went deeper than that. Much deeper.

'What am I doing here? Who the hell am I?'

The dry broken croak must be his own voice. He didn't recognize it. If he had ever been more frightened or desperate he could not remember it. He could not remember anything.

He put his right hand up to scratch a stiffness running up the back of his neck to his head, and when he looked at his fingers the nails were clotted with dried blood. His hands searched the area gently and found what felt like a large area of the dried blood and a swelling like a duck's egg.

He stayed there trying to remember.

It was useless.

His name had gone. His identity, the reality which was himself, the individual man, was lost somewhere in the hurting confused heat inside his head. Only one word was in his mind: Alex. Alex? It meant nothing to him.

Why was he here in this silent peaceful sunlit emptiness with three dead men? He held his hands out in front of him and stared at them carefully. With three dead men whose skins were darker than his own?

He had a sudden desire to run. Away to some place which must be familiar. Away from rising fear. Away from sickness which came and went but never brought relief. Away from dead men on whom the ants feasted.

Where to?

For what?

To whom?

Alex.

Alex?

He narrowed his eyes and turned towards the sunlit hillside opposite, wincing as his dirty gritty bloodied hand folded on his forehead. It burned like a hot iron. For a long moment full of dread he feared some horrible . . . event? event had bashed his skull in and done permanent damage to his brain. He heard himself moan. Then instinct aided him. He could use his hands and legs. He could stand. He knew the nature of his fear. No man whose brain had sustained irreparable damage could do those things as . . .

Concussion.

Amnesia.

Words. Words with meaning. Many men who were concussed could not remember anything when they regained consciousness. And he could reason though on a very low level.

His fingers searched his injured head.

Alex?

It meant nothing.

He lowered his hands, wondering what to do. He stood up, turned slowly full circle, his aching eyes down to tiny slits as he tried to see if he had been mistaken and there was any sign of people or a house, and he sat down again. There were neither. Only when he glanced up at the sky did he detect anything new: several large birds wheeled silently, watching the dead men and the gluttonous ants. He looked down.

He was alone. It felt familiar to him. His right hand went to his hip and to under his left shoulder. It found nothing. It should have found something hard . . . a weapon. An automatic. There had been an automatic . . . everything had gone. A rucksack on his back . . . the fire on the ground. Only what he wore, a safari jacket over an old khaki-coloured shirt, substantial grey trousers covered in dust and spattered with blood, woollen socks, heavy shoes with metal-studded soles. That was . . . no. An ancient hat lay where he had regained consciousness.

How did he know it was a safari jacket? What did safari mean? Alex.

Something else. Coming, no, going going.

Bell!

Bell? What bell? That felt wrong in his aching head. Which bell? Alex Bell?

It might be.

A worn safari jacket and grubby trousers. And three dead men. And a fire.

That was wrong. There must be something else. He had a recollection of talking to someone as they walked towards where the sun had been moving. Or was that fantasy? Things slid in and out of his mind without his being aware of them until they had passed, like fish which had come from the gloom and flicked away. Fantasy.

He gazed at the emptiness. No man walked through this sort of country without purpose. To reach somewhere. Where he might come from was another matter. It could be any one of a thousand villages or towns separated by one sort of desert or other with only a few trees.

Desert. *Wadis.* Bedu: Arabs, Tuaregs with hawk faces protected by wound blue . . . face-clothes.

He gazed at the ground. No wheel tracks had dug a pattern into this soil. No camels had come here. This was mountain country far from deserts which made him feel good.

Again he slitted his eyes to look at the radiant sky. More of the birds circled overhead. By now wild dogs if nothing else had seen the birds and read their meaning correctly. Hungry wild dogs were fiercer than birds.

Suddenly he was violently sick, retching on after the vile-smelling stuff had left him. He waited for another bout of dizziness to go and when it did so he searched the dead men methodically. Their pockets were empty. They wore no rings or identity-tags or loop of cord around the neck. The cartridges which killed them were larger than usual . . . cartridges? His own pockets were empty. Nothing gave a clue to his identity.

He stood up unsteadily. He felt thirsty, his sour tongue big in his mouth. He had a feeling that someone was watching him. But the hill slopes, the valley, the clump of trees, were empty. Only one thing had changed. The waiting birds had started to settle around him on the ground, watching him.

After some terrible moments of indecision he started to walk on towards the unseen sun. For all he knew he might be going in entirely the wrong direction. It did not matter. He felt lightheaded. At times his sight blurred over and his head was always being sawn through and his legs still felt weak. Gusts of sourness came up from his stomach without bringing relief.

On several occasions he veered off the track but managed to find it again. The important thing was to keep going. He knew that but he did not know why he knew it.

It must have been an hour later that he thought one of his beliefs was proven true. By then he had discovered he was wearing a watch and he wondered why.

He was nearing the end of the valley when it turned abruptly left. Sunlight was fading. Shadows lengthened. Separate colours merged on the hillsides. His thirst had increased steadily. In a sick sort of way he had begun to feel hungry. Occasionally his head felt about to take off like a balloon, empty of everything, then he felt pain stab through it again. Frequent bouts of nerves troubled him. That felt strange; he never suffered from nerves or what was the modern term? stress? Twice he stopped abruptly as a sort of half-curtain of blazing lights floated in front of his eyes.

It happened soon after he went on from the second stop.

He was close to another wood which spread across the track.

Now he walked better, his legs gaining strength. Without reason he glanced up the hillside on his left to where a shaft of reddening sunlight slanted down across the earth and two nests of smooth boulders like huge prehistoric eggs left by some monster. On one boulder a woman sat watching him.

At first he thought it must be another hallucination of a mind which could not remember and did not know and could not put words and thoughts together. She sat motionless. Her arms were straight down at her sides for her hands to hold her steady, her legs were in front of her with the left across the right at the knee, her naked feet balanced on another boulder or so he thought. A mane of chestnut-coloured hair covered her shoulders. He could not see her face, hidden in shadow cast by her hair. She seemed to be wearing a dark ankle-length dress of some dark colour, gathered at the waist and with a great slack fold over her breasts and stomach.

He stood still wondering what to do. Then he called to her, telling her to wait, and started to climb towards her. The going proved harder than he expected, partly on account of weakness, partly because of the ground and the thin air. After some minutes he raised his head to call again.

The woman had vanished. Sunlight illuminated the boulders but there was no one there. He climbed more rapidly, anxious and disappointed.

When he got to the boulders the woman had vanished. No clue, not even a hair, provided proof of a woman having been there. He passed a hand over the surface of each boulder on which she might have sat but it proved a useless exercise; his hand found no extra warmth or lack of dust. After he called out the air remained silent until a faint, eerie echo of his own voice drifted back from the opposite hillside.

Uneasily he turned and inspected the boulders again though he knew they would tell him nothing. He had this unknown valley to himself. The shape of a woman had been a delusion caused by the sunlight.

After a while he started to descend the darkening hill, heading diagonally for a point on the track near the next wedge of trees. It proved awkward, his feet slithering among stones and rocks in patches of long thin shadow. The half-light and other things unsettled him. His headache was worse again, possibly from disappointment and the effort of climbing the hillside. His thirst had increased steadily and hunger was a twisting sick ache in his stomach. Above all he felt tired and fuddled, worn by failure to remember who he was and why he came here.

Near the trail again he stumbled over a large stone and fell full-length. He lay panting, dust thick on his tongue, the first anguish sawing inside his head again. It seemed beyond his strength to pick himself off the ground. Dully he supposed everyone at some time had his longing now to just die and have done with confusion and aches and fright.

When eventually he managed to haul himself off the ground he regretted it instantly. Another shining bead-curtain of electric light-bulbs like a migraine covered the top half of his vision so that he could only look down to where his feet seemed to swim in the thickening gloom. He managed to stay upright though he felt himself swaying in a swirling world.

'A fine bloody carry on,' he snarled savagely. 'If it isn't one goddam bloody thing it's another.'

He walked on more unsteadily. As he reached the dark wood, now too dark for him to see clearly, he had his first bit of luck. He halted to listen, unwilling to trust his ears after the trick played on his eyes. The sound went on and on without pause and was not far ahead of him: the steady plash of water falling over stones somewhere inside the wood.

Cautious and fumbling, he managed to make his way among the trees heading towards the sound, afraid lest it might suddenly fade from his ears. It did not do so. Unbelievably the moment came when he lay on his stomach to sip cautiously. The flowing water was ice-cold, beautiful in his mouth and throat. He had never tasted anything more exquisite. In an existence of which no detail lay in his mind now it had been thought unwise to drink too much chill water on an empty stomach and after prolonged thirst, so he did not drink so deeply as he wanted.

He sluiced his face and neck. Carefully he sat up again. The lights still blazed before his aching eyes, his head was still being sawn, but he felt easier.

No sound came to him.

Now he admitted to extreme tiredness. Most probably it came from a combination of having his strength sapped and from keeping tension and fear under control. At this time he had to rationalize every psychological tendency or he knew that he would lose his nerve.

Here it was beautifully quiet. He found no strangeness or dread alone here in this darkness. Surely that was unusual? Most people hated to be alone. Yet even with a blank mind he found it preferable to being surrounded by people. Unusual?

What sort of man was he to accept aloneness as . . . ordinary?

Alex.

Alec?

No, Alex.

It still meant nothing.

After some minutes he had another short drink to sweeten his mouth and then got to his feet. He couldn't see anything except jagged narrow patches of darkness among the tangle of branches overhead. Ah! The migraine sensation was wearing off. Good!

'Good. Good? What language is this? Good?'

He buried his face in his hands.

'Pull yourself together,' he whispered, and lowered his hands. 'Now what shall I do?'

It would be useless to go on. All animals slept at night. And he needed to regain strength; he might have a long walk ahead on an empty stomach, a day, more.

He turned on his heels and held his arm out in front of him. One unsure step at a time he edged forward until his right hand collided with a tree-trunk. He felt it carefully while his other hand searched wide around him without finding anything. Reassured, he turned until his back found the tree and he sat down using it as a prop.

He knew he must stay awake. It had been wrong to think all animals slept at night. Predators and night marauders of every specie were always active during darkness, using it to cover them as they moved in to kill their quarry. But here he should be safe. He would hear them coming. And if he stayed awake the darkness might help him to remember.

He went to sleep.

A stiffness in his neck awoke him. He sat up to ease his back and hips. It took several minutes to manipulate the stiffness out of his neck. While he did so he saw that a full moon had arisen. Its radiance penetrated between branches and put patches of bright or pale light on strips of ground all around him. None were near him. The trickling murmur of the stream put a gentle, companionable note into the night.

His mind jerked to a halt.

Murmur.

Murmur?

It meant nothing to him, nothing he could remember.

He looked up through the branches at the moon and saw it was not full, only half full, the illusion being caused by leaves and branches. He looked down and listened to the murmur of the stream, a more pleasant sound than the far away howl of some wild dog. As his eyes grew accustomed to the gloom he thought he could see a human shape lying half in and half out of a pool of moonlight alongside a tree some yards over on his left, just across the stream. This time he did not let himself be fooled though as he yawned aloud and stretched his arms he thought the shape raised the silhouette of a head several inches from the ground as if looking towards him. He ignored it. He had seen a woman who did not exist, a full moon had days to reach that stage. Only a fool let himself get the screaming hab-dabs by imagining a trunk or fallen branch was human.

He twisted his neck and eased his shoulders several times and then settled down and went to sleep again.

When he awoke again the sun had already risen clear of the hills on his right. Although it was still early morning he could feel the first warmth of a new day's heat inside the wood. No sound reached him. He stayed where he was, willing what he used for a mind to awaken slowly, without a rush which could renew his headache or bring disappointment, letting it tell him what it could of its own volition. It had nothing to tell him. Except that he was ravenously hungry, down to the level where men chewed the bark of trees to gain an illusion of eating food. And his body ached more sharply now than it had done yesterday.

That pleased him. One little segment of memory stirred in him. Oh, I remember yesterday . . . it sounded like the words of a song.

He glanced at the place across the stream where he thought he had seen a body on the ground during the night. It wasn't there now. There was nothing there. Not even a log or fallen branch. He glanced at adjacent trees. The ground at the base of each bole showed no trace of a log or branch.

Another illusion, he told himself.

He started to prepare himself for the day to prevent a tendency to brood over his plight. He took off the hat he must have worn all night for it was still on his head though he had forgotten putting it there. Next, carefully, he got to his feet and took a careful jump across the stream, turned to get his bearing on the place where he had left his hat, and started to search. It did not take long. Within moments he found a tree at whose foot some weight had lain and twisted on old leaves during the night, breaking their stalks and folding them with its pressure. He could almost make out the shape of a body. His gaze travelled along it and beyond to where feet had scuffed leaves aside as they stood there. So he had been right on one point at least. Someone had been watching him yesterday.

Now everything was quiet again. Once again no movement attracted his eyes. And the air was as empty of birdsong as the branches were free of disturbance by fluttering wings.

He drew a long deep breath and knew it was clean high-up air, which meant he must know the difference between it and the air at lower levels. So he did not think he was a native here. Besides his skin was paler than that of those three dead men he left with the birds and ants yesterday.

Suddenly he was full of anxiety, hopeless, overwhelmed by uncertainty about what to do. Unsure, robbed of purpose, he lay down beside the stream and washed the taste of hunger out of his mouth. He swilled his face and neck, swallowed several mouthfuls of water, and then plunged his whole head into the stream to wash away the dust and the dried blood matting hair at the back and tight on his neck. It took some time to get rid of the dried blood; the lump on his head seemed less than he remembered it. He took off his safari jacket and shirt and splashed icy water over his chest and arms, let it trickle down his back, washing himself to the waist and drying off with his shirt. The simple tasks helped to lessen his tension. When he finished a measure of hope crept into him.

He sat beside his drying shirt with his legs drawn up, trying to think.

What had he been thinking about before he washed? Something about being overwhelmed by uncertainty?

Overwhelmed?

'Overwhelmed him with her beauty'?

Alex.

'Overwhelm racial prejudice'?

He thought for some time. Then he stood up, shaking his head gently. At first it had seemed as if his mind was poised on the verge of memory, a complete clarification of the fog of emptiness inside his head. But, again, nothing.

Despondent and weary, he carried his shirt and jacket back across the stream.

Already the morning was warm enough for him not to feel the air cold on his naked chest and back. He knelt down beside his ancient hat and went still, gazing at it. In his absence the hat had been turned upside-down: inside it were walnuts, a cluster of grapes, three apricots. Someone was watching him. His eyes had not misled him. And the someone was not a man. Only a woman, a primitive woman he guessed though one whose instinct knew human need in an unknown man which raised her above fear and uncertainty, only a woman would do this like this. But it might not be quite so simple. Suspicion seemed natural to him, he realised. Every mousetrap was baited with cheese. It did not matter. This mouse was hungry.

He started to eat one of the apricots. It was full of juicy fruit and sweet on his tongue. No fruit had ever tasted better.

3

Suddenly midway through the morning he hurried to a boulder
and sat down on it and put his head in his hands. Instantly he
forced open his eyes and raised his head again although nausea
swirled round his stomach and smeared sickness on his tongue.
Without conscious effort memory had started to trickle into his
mind. Now it seemed to rush through his head like a river in
torrent. It made him dizzy and confused. He looked round at
the sunlit emptiness in a desperate effort to borrow something
of its quietness to keep calm.

He had walked for nearly three hours without seeing anyone.
Yes. Around him the whole world seemed empty under a
cloudless sky. Yes. Heat in the valley rose steadily. Yes. The
opposite hillside reflected it down towards his tiny solitary
figure. Yes. There had been no sign of his mysterious benefac-
tress. She was somewhere out of sight but near to him, using her
local knowledge to remain unseen for whatever motives
prompted her. Yes?

At some point he must have gone wrong. That implied he
knew where he was and knew the right way. He did not. Everything was strange. But at seven or eight places the track had
divided into two, each break a narrow footpath worn by the
feet of people who had passed along them over the years. In
some places the paths were so unused that they almost disappeared in thin dingy grass or stretches of dust. He had avoided
them and kept to the worn tracks.

As he walked his thirst and hunger returned. So did his head-ache, though it was easier. Then, a few paces away from this boulder, he told himself he must have faith that he would regain his memory, above all faith. His mind had seized on the word faith. And it transformed it into Fathiya.

It was a small change in itself. To others it would have meant nothing. To him Fathiya meant a woman. A very beautiful woman, to his eyes the most beautiful woman from crown of head to soles of feet, the most exquisitely lovely being, he ever knew. She had one acquisition which to other women had proved a hellish curse: money. No one knew now how much money she had but by present standards it was well over fifty millions. If she had been a fool it would have surrounded her with life-long dearest friends in for the pickings, the sort of people who were a purgatory in every city and at every fashion-able resort where they went scavenging.

Fathiya. The yacht she had given him for them to mess about in away from hangers-on and which he had returned to her ownership without her knowledge. Fathiya. A yacht. Himself. A man named...Priest? Monk? Priest. Yes, Priest. And his own name...Silk! Darius Silk? No...no...no. Dorian. Dorian Silk.

The effort to think on made him feel sick but he stayed there forcing himself to watch the torrent of memory flooding through his mind.

Fathiya and he had gone on holiday. They boarded the yacht at Genoa and sailed round . . . the foot of Italy and across the bottom of the sea . . . the . . . the sea which divided . . . Greece from Turkey? Turkey had been their goal. Their small crew was English. Fathiya was Egyptian. He had people who had crewed with him before and she brought along the woman cook and butler, a married couple, from her home in England.

He cursed in exasperation. It was coming through disjoint-edly. He had to get it into sequence.

He began again . . . and Turkey was their goal. They had been unable to have a holiday together for two or three years. At the very end of the winter—now that England did without a spring—he took a mini-sabbatical for three months. So they were together again enjoying being together in the role of tramps which suited them best, away from eyes and fawning voices and mainstream holipack crowds, the photographers which settled like vultures around every rich woman and an unknown companion. And they got to Turkey and sailed slowly north up the coast. They put in overnight at one port or another, usually the small ones which provided anonymity. They sailed through the . . . Dardanelles and the . . . Sea of . . . Marmite, Fathiya called it . . . Marmara! . . . to Constantin . . . Istanbul. Yes, Istanbul. They went to see something. A link? A link. A new bridge . . . across the Bosphorus which linked Europe and the Near East by land, the Bosphorus Bridge. They trippered around Istanbul for some days, a beautiful city with a touch of Venice along the waterside where the old aristocracy, the *yalis*, once lived. Nobody knew them. Nobody cared two hoots about them. Marvellous!

Right! He was on course now.

They sailed south again through the Hellespont—the Dardanelles—to . . . Izmir.

He frowned, momentarily lost. Izmir. A rough ride inland in a jeep on a hot day. His mind cleared again. They had gone to the city known to the ancient world as Aphrodisias, one of the great art centres of antiquity until it was destroyed by successive earthquakes and its terrified survivors dispersed, their culture ruined and forgotten. They spent three weeks there with American professors and students working on excavations and reconstruction. Every day they sweated side by side in a plot between a stadium and the Temple of Aphrodite. Every day they worked till dusk. They discovered the battered stone head of a goddess which the students thought might be a copy of

Alcamenes's *Aphrodite of the Gardens*, or a lost Astarte. Then they jolted back up the hot dusty road to Izmir and the yacht.

No bed ever felt so voluptuous. They enjoyed it superbly together. Later Fathiya had said: 'We should do this more often.'

'Criticisms, criticisms.'

'No, *güzel*.'

'Where did you pick up that word?'

'I talked to a Turk. He got a bit amorous and told me I am beautiful.'

'Must have been tight.'

'My very own male chauvinist pig,' she said affectionately, and tried to wound him with a knee which lacked malice. 'No, I meant this sort of holiday. Particularly this. I find this much more satisfying than feeling like something kept on hand to be warmed up for a compulsory snack at the end of an evening. A sort of female supfast.'

'How disgusting! Roe on toast! Have I ever made you feel like that?'

'Allah forbid!' she exclaimed at the start of a rush of Arabic, and then checked herself. 'No, you make me feel like a big whoosh of music.'

He felt contrite. 'Only a Muslima would put up with the sort of life you have because you're dotty enough to like me,' he said.

She laid fingers over his mouth. 'You've never tried to take my money and you won't even live off it,' she said. 'There aren't many honest men about.'

'It's the inflation.'

'I get so frightened that something terrible will happen to you and I won't be there to pick up the pieces.'

He felt the shiver which went through her. 'Good friends of mine will tell you I was in lots of pieces until you picked me up in Cairo,' he told her.

'Honest?'

'Cross my heart.'

'What do they think of you now?'

'They say I'm almost bearable.'

She laughed quietly. 'I like to enjoy my accomplishments . . .' she said as if offering something.

Late the next day Priest joined them on the yacht unexpectedly.

He stood up and turned round a couple of times and sat down again. Even the sound of her voice rang clear in his mind. Memory after memory flooded through him. They caused only a slight headache.

Priest had said: 'The sun has caught you,' Fathiya had left them alone for their brandy after dinner. 'You could easily be mistaken for an Arab.'

'Don't tell Gaddafi.'

'Actually you look rather like him.'

'Poor him. Did you come here to strew compliments over me? Or does the House of Lords bore you?'

'The speeches there are better than those in the other place.'

'How intensely difficult. Carry on.'

'We need someone to undertake a simple little jaunt in Pakistan,' Priest told him.

Priest was his London-based superior in what people still called M.I.6, or 'the old firm' or SIS, Special Intelligence Service. It was the foreign wing of intelligence, collecting information abroad on events likely to affect British security; mercifully, it had little to do with that strange set-up M.I.5, home-based counter-intelligence, which everyone knew was a home for retired policemen. Priest and Silk had known each other since youth.

Over the years their mutual trust had deepened to the farthest point possible between an agent who risked his life on every foreign mission and a controller who relied on a field agent not to betray him and other agents in a network. The bond between them had some personal involvement. Silk knew Priest's wife and their children. Priest knew Fathiya and about her incredible wealth. The safety of both women, and Priest's children, depended on their personal integrity in an age when that quality was largely ignored or derided.

Priest's appearance had been unexpected. It was without warning. Secret agents seldom sought each other out while one or other was off-duty. The 'simple little jaunt' sounded unlikely.

Here, sitting on this boulder in a high empty valley, he could hear the incredulity in his voice as he asked: 'How simple?'

'Well . . .'

'Ah! Truth will out. Go on.'

'We have a man stationed in one of the Black Kafir valleys. Gervase Bell. An artist. Have you met him?'

'Indeed. We shared some tricky days together. Twice? Yes, twice. How do you maintain contact?'

'Radio.'

'Leaving out simplicity, how significant is it? I've a few weeks' holiday in hand.'

Priest nodded as if the thought struck a faint chime. 'Briefly, the politico-military situation in Pakistan has not settled down since the Bangladesh matter,' he said. 'The army is smarting at what it regards as unjustified criticism. The country has problems. Baluchi separatists and Pushtu irredentists have revived their campaigns. Both want to join the western half of the country to Afghanistan. Every few weeks, sometimes every few days, we hear rumours of quarrels among the new politicians in power. Economic problems due to climate and neglect and temperament are no help. Those fools. People dislike so many Western Pakistan troops from Bangladesh still being locked up in Indian POW camps. They blame the Prime Minister.'

'I thought he took Pakistan out of the Commonwealth. How are we involved?'

'Remember your geopolitics. There's more at stake than miffed politicians. And that goes for everywhere at present with Brezhnev fooling far too may people that it'll be hearts and flowers forever if only . . . you believe this?'

'I'm not a politician. I look at the length of my spoon before I sup with a fiend. Tell me more about Bell.'

'He stays in the valley most of the time. Occasionally he goes to Karachi or Rawalpindi to get essential supplies or to get in touch with us. He enjoys the solitary existence.'

'A woman?'

'He dislikes them.'

'Poor him. They're so nicely different and unpredictable. What does he do?'

'He paints landscapes. It helps him climb hills to a high place to send messages.'

'Are the tribal people inquisitive?'

'They were at first. They've accepted him since he learned their language.'

Silk was puzzled. 'No woman?' he queried. 'Most artists need one around for a woman to put the size of the landscape into perspective. A woman is a better model than a man. She twitches less.'

'I always forget you were one once.'

'Have you seen his work?'

'No. But I've sent him materials, brushes, canvases, tubes of paint.'

'What colours?'

'Oh, umber, a sort of russet, other browns, a green beginning with v.'

'Viridian. What reds?'

'Madder? A sort of damask, rose, carmine, vermilion.'

'Did you send him much white?'

'Quite a lot.'

'Not only the hills painted he,' Silk said and explained how its usage robbed colour of heat. 'You learn something every day,' he said politely. 'Any other away-from-it-all folk there?'

'None. We checked regularly.'

'Now, what does Bell do there, apart from paint?'

'Report on developments among the separatists. He has lately reported regular flights of unidentified aircraft crossing into Pakistan airspace from a northwesterly direction. On two occasions he saw parachutes come down. Subsequently he found the remains of a broken crate and its stuffing. Some stuffing had thick grease on it.'

'And now?'

'We don't know. He started his last five calls on schedule and was immediately jammed. On the last three he switched to a standby wavelength and was jammed again.'

Silk poured them brandies and did a thunk.

'I know your interest in ancient history,' Priest said after some moments, 'so I thought you'd be ideal for the job. Particularly as you're halfway there. You can finish your holiday directly you get back.'

Silk finished his brandy slowly while he thought. His decision affected Fathiya as much as himself. She had dropped everything for them to be together for this holiday; she always did. She understood him too acutely to complain. She was too affectionate and loyal to raise objections to his working as a 'reporter' for the news-agency of which Priest was part owner.

'Can I let you know in the morning?' he asked finally.

'Of course,' Priest agreed, He stood up. 'You've fed me too well.'

'Agreed.'

'Do I detect an acid note?'

'One guess.'

As Silk entered their cabin Fathiya lay on their bunk looking exotically elegant in nothing. The black sheet and scarlet

42

pillows ensured that her smoky bronze did not escape attention. She gave him a penetrating look and a calm smile.

'I shall name him as co-respondent,' she announced without bitterness as she laid aside the *Telegraph* crossword. 'When do you leave?'

'I haven't decided to go yet.'

'When?' she repeated.

'Three or four days. If I go.'

'Let's enjoy them.'

He sat down and let his hand admire her. 'When didn't we?' he queried.

'I really have become very sensual,' she announced. 'This is much more than nice . . . he is a nice man, I'm fond of him and Louise and the children. But I wish he hadn't come here.' She sat up and twined her arms round him. 'Let's forget him and people and everything.'

He smiled foolishly as he sat there on the boulder and felt sweat trickle down his forehead and neck. They had forgotten. They always did.

He glanced round at the empty hillsides. The distant snow-caps rising above the northern hillside looked familiar. They should be. Priest had briefed him thoroughly.

His memory went on. He had seen Fathiya off on her return flight to England and promised they should finish their holiday on their particular Greek island directly he finished his reporting job. Then he saw Priest take off on his return flight. He watched the crew sail the yacht out of harbour.

And then?

His head started to ache wildly again.

He flew to Cyprus? Yes. He flew to Cyprus.

Then?

Then? What then? What did he do after he got to Cyprus?

Eden! Priest had said that on this mission he should be Doctor David Eden, an archeologist using a holiday for a visit

to an old artist friend who lived in a valley south of the Hindu
Kush near to where Alexander the Great had marched long ago.

Alex—Alexander the Great. Of course! Alex the overwhelmed man!

He had a fading recollection of telling someone about Alex.
He had flown from Cyprus to Karachi.

What happened then? What had he done? How did he get
here?

Gone.

It was gone completely. It might come back, it would come
back one day, but now, no, gone. Snippets of memory like thin
smoke drifted over his mind. A narrow *la*, a mountain pass,
like those high up in Tibet. A typical glacier, *gol*, the water still
icy. Successive memories or bits from now and much earlier
mixed up in his vague memory.

He wiped sweat off his neck. This was the Valley of Drahozi.
Yes, he remembered that. Ahead of him was Dukanis Pass
leading to the Black Kafir Valley of Turikrun. Where Bell
lived. Only a few miles away. He opened his mouth to suck
in air and lessen the stale taste of hunger which had begun to
give him another stomachache. No doubt Bell would give him
a good evening meal; every artist he knew found lunch an
irritation but enjoyed a good supper after the light had gone.
The Valley of Drahozi. Dukanis Pass. Turikrun. Gervase Bell.
That was not his real name but the one under which he lived.
He wiped his neck again.

He hissed angrily. It was useless. Try as he might, he could
not remember a blind thing about what happened after he
got on the plane at Cyprus. He must have gone to Chitral to
get here but he could not remember how or where he stopped.
A typical case of temporary amnesia. He had completely
forgotten the immediate past.

After some moments he got to his feet. As he looked round
at emptiness he put on his ancient hat, tipping it forward to
keep the glare out of his aching eyes. Then he drew several

deep breaths and started on towards Dukanis Pass and the Valley of Turikrun. Bell would fill in the holes for him. Once he found Bell he would sort himself out.

An hour later he came in sight of the pass.

While he walked the ground had descended slightly and become more fertile. He had left behind the wide patches of bare ground, mostly grit mixed with a form of sand, broken by tiny pockets where seed had chanced on blown soil and germinated to produce tufts of coarse grass. Gone too were the slopes of bare rock. Over large stretches of ground here lay coverings of topsoil which sustained still succulent green grass. Little copses on the valley floor and lower slopes of the hillsides had thickened into sizeable woods; he had forgotten the names of the trees if he ever knew them but the numerous bushes, some with little white or dark red flowers, had a profusion of small oblong crinkly dark leaves similar to pittasporum. There were more goats than he had seen previously. He saw other signs of people though he had not seen any. Still, it would not be long now before he found Bell in the Valley of Turikrun.

He had kept repeating the names in his mind to ensure they did not slip out of sight.

At the verge of the wood at the bottom of the pass he sat down on a boulder to get his breath. It was a large wood, patched with sunlight where trees had been hewn. He admitted to feeling a bit tired after a long slow day spent mainly on his feet. At times his headache had hammered viciously but for the last couple of hours it had dwindled to a subdued pulse which only bothered him at odd moments. But he needed these moments to renew his two roles of eager archaeologist and watchful observer. Whatever the next few hours brought he could not risk being unprepared. A man without a gun had little chance in some corners of the world. This might be one of them. He needed whatever wits he could find.

A near movement caused him to look up. It was a bit late to

acknowledge a need of wits. He had been caught napping.

Too near him stood a man with an unfriendly sort of dagger gripped purposefully. The man had two male companions. A third companion was the woman he had seen sitting on a boulder in half-light and who he believed had fed him nuts and fruit. The other men also had Asian type knives, fanciful gadgets which resembled a snake coiling along the ground, probably a reminder of the cult of Naga snake-worshippers. At a distance of less than twenty paces he saw that the woman was a girl by Western standards, not more than twenty, though that made her a full-grown woman in these regions. She provided more interest than mere age: living proof that at some time white men had come here, probably the legion of Alexander. She was a fair-skinned Black Kafir with deep chest-nut-coloured hair and pointed thin features, tall, her figure pure speculation under a brown robe with a heavy slack fold across her chest and stomach and with its hemline down to her heels. Her large blue eyes had a glint of excitement.

The men were equally interesting. They were Europeans of some variety; perhaps the American description of Caucasian would be more accurate. At first sight they looked wild types, like the more politically active students who sought to impress with their hair as much as their ism. The nearest man had a great mop of untidy dark hair which stood high on his head, sprang out like lively bushes above each ear, covered his upper lip and jaw, and came halfway down his chest in a thick spade-shaped beard which would be useful for birds in the nesting season. Obviously the face beneath this lot gave him feelings of intense inferiority. At present, under riotous dark eyebrows, his milk-chocolate brown eyes had an affronted gleam. Somewhere below his fleshy nose the hair started to part.

Silk got in first. 'Good afternoon, gentlemen,' he said sunnily. 'Warm, isn't it?'

4

They looked at him.

Their looking went on long enough to have the atmosphere of a strip of elastic being slowly stretched. Silk knew that the men understood what he had said. Their eyes had registered comprehension of the words he used. Nonetheless they were content to stare at him as if they needed a long time to decide on how precisely they should express their delight at meeting him apart from this flourish of ceremonial knives. Two of them were vacant of eye as if preoccupied by matters of highest importance. They gave the appearance of having drifted into the scene, the knives in their hands dangling like unused tooth-picks at an Asian banquet. On a not entirely unrelated point, Silk was relieved to find that in an emergency he could muster sufficient energy to take one form of initiative. He had seldom met other people so easily nonplussed. Particularly when they had the only weapons available.

Once again he saw a ripple through the beard-smothered face which looked like the first stage of a surgical operation. Perhaps it involved a good deal of physical effort. The beard alone would stuff a bolster. He pursued his slight and temporary advantage.

'Perhaps you gentlemen can assist me,' he said chattily as if they had been discussing the local flora and fauna for hours,'and the lady too, of course.' It went against his grain to get down to the idiocy of calling a woman a lady but these types might have their tiny dignity about etiquette. 'I believe that beyond the pass is Turikrun Valley.'

'No!' came from the Beard.

'Yes,' chorused the other two men.

The woman offered no contribution.

'I see,' Silk said, 'It leads to it.' The smile on his face had begun to ache like a dying nerve in a tooth. 'It leads to it, yes. How far is it from here? Roughly?'

They reverted to their previous enchantment with non-communication which gave him an opportunity to absorb a few more details about them. The other two bore a similarity of personality but none shared positive physical characteristics. One was a tubby man of about five four or five in height. Whenever he moved his fat tended to wobble and ripple alarmingly. He had a type of chin-fringe beard, fashionable a hundred years ago among young Afrikaner farmers and now the pride of many a campus. He wore a thin, pale blue cotton shirt which had enjoyed better health and flared lilac slacks still waiting for it. The third man was taller and thinner than either of his companions, and had tidier if greasier hair of a hue somewhere between brown and black. His pale sunken face was not cheered up by a Mexican peon gravy-dipper moustache; it gave him some similarity to a suburban undertaker or a film cowboy villain. He wore a shirt of broad vertical stripes of purple and orange and black and scarlet with skin-tight lime green slacks; evidently he was afraid his friends might miss him. Both he and the tubby man wore Middle East sandals of red leather.

The Beard was all in black. In brief gaps between the growths of hair his skin was darkly weather-tanned. The other two might have been gay liberation bit-actors and were of no consequence except that they looked likely to do whatever they were told, without thinking about it, a fashionable twentieth-century disease of the mind. The Beard was different. He had a rugged authority and his eyes held anger and malice

and a glint of wildness which hinted at a violent and unpredictable temper if he let himself get going. Silk thought that
might not be a hard struggle.

He had to play it on the ear even if he got little co-operation.

'Perhaps you gentlemen come from another valley,' he said
amiably, and giggled like a lonely man unused to easy conversation. 'There seem to be quite a lot. It must be very confusing.
Ahmmmmm yes.'

The Beard found his voice. 'What are you doing here? 'he
demanded aggressively.

'As I indicated, I want to find Turikrun Valley.'

'Why?'

The Dude Peon had a voice. 'Yeh,' he added. 'Why?' His
voice was thin, scratchy as an old record.

Silk nodded amiably. 'I am Doctor Eden,' he said, 'Doctor
David Eden.' He gave a little self-conscious smirk and glanced
at each of them in turn as if he expected everyone alive to
recognize the name instantly. 'Archaeology, y' know,' he added
as if still hopeful of being known and admired, still smiling;
with no response, he decided to build it out. 'Television, that
sort of thing. A regular series. I'm searching for places for my
next series . . . ahmmmmm, no, I don't suppose they get this
far, not from London.' Their eyes remained completely blank.
Yet he had a feeling he had dropped the coin in the right slot;
a missing television personality was more newsworthy search
material than a pretty nurse or an average tourist, Allah knew
why. 'Well, an old friend of mine lives in the valley and he
thought it might be helpful to see it,' he resumed in his best
world-famous television notoriety voice. 'So friends brought
me part of the way here – helicopters are so helpful, aren't they?
– and they're going to pick me up after I've seen my friend.
That's why I want to find the valley.'

It might be that they had difficulty in understanding things
or that the high air kept their minds drowsy. Long minutes
passed while they digested the information. The Tub

and the Dude Peon left it to the Beard to renew contact.

'You have a friend,' he slid as a question seeking guidance.

'Ahmmmmmm, yes, yes. One here, several in Chitral.'

'The friend you want to see lives in Turikrun Valley.'

'Yes. Yes.'

'What friend in Turikrun?'

He tch–tched petulance. 'An Englishman,' he said in a tone calculated to wither roses. 'An artist.'

'There's no English artist in Turikrun,' the Beard said, and nodded his hair to show agreement with himself. 'You're wasting your time. You'd better go back to Chitral now.'

'You are wrong,' Silk said and got to his feet, easing his shoulders in case open defiance precipitated assault. 'He was here a few weeks ago. I had a letter which he posted in Chitral. That's why I'm here.'

Momentarily the Beard looked uneasy. Then a latent intelligence gave him an idea. 'Have you got it with you?' he demanded brusquely.

Silk did not fall for it. 'I left it at my hotel in Chitral,' he answered mildly. 'With my friends,' He was sure now that something had happened in the valley, something which came under the heading of the expected unexpected, the sort of thing which an agent hoped would never happen and often did. He glanced at the silent woman and saw her face was expressionless, her eyes studying him carefully. 'You may not recognise my friend as an Englishman or an artist,' he said.

'Why not?'

'You know how famous artists are in their habits. Many like to keep their identity and work a secret. Not all, but quite a number. They dislike having their privacy invaded by reporters or people who interrupt their work routine.' He gave another self-conscious little smirk, tinged with regret. 'We old television hands are more used to it than most people nowadays, of course. Interviews, y' know, the penalty of being what some people regard as a celebrity. So many people get to know us . . .

why, even in Chitral a few days ago a man and his wife came up and told me they had seen my programme in England or America or somewhere. It's the curse of the media. We have to accept it as our fate.'

While he indulged his secret weapon of chat the men were working up a fine old tension. He could tell it from their eyes and foreheads. He doubted if any of them had much skill in disciplining their faces; perhaps that was the reason for their facial adornments, a partial disguise. Thank Heaven, loquacity had not yet deserted him. It had not helped much except as a delaying factor. He gathered the impression that these men wanted to keep him away from Turikrun. Their clumsy attempt only awoke his curiosity and foreboding.

To his partial relief the Beard put his dagger into a sheath on the heavy belt secured round his waist by a big silver buckle. Immediately the other two men put their daggers away.

The Beard was one of those men who needed some time to think of what to say next. It was probably no more than a few seconds but it seemed much longer. Silk smiled at the girl. His attempt to charm shattered like thin glass on a concrete wall.

The Beard blew heavily down his nose. It caused the hair below to ripple like corn in a strong wind. Silk detected exasperation.

'What's your friend's name?' the man demanded.

Silk played it coy. 'Perhaps I've talked too much about him already,' he said worriedly, 'Some people loathe having their identity known. And their whereabouts. 'I don't. I'm sure he is in the valley, Mr . . . ? What did you say your name is?'

The Tub scowled at him. 'Why do you want to know –' he began.

The Beard interrupted. 'Hawks,' he said curtly. 'Oliver Hawks. And you are . . . ?'

'As I said, Doctor David Eden. And these friends of yours . . . ?'

'Francis Hawkins and John Becket,' the Beard told him,

nodding first at the Tub. When he spoke normally he had a cultured sort of voice, easy, soft. His change of tone might be due to uncertainty. 'I'm sure you're wrong, Doctor Eden. I've never heard of him. There's no English artist at Turikrun. But you'd better come and see for yourself.'

'Why the hell should he –' the Tub began.

'You know what we were told,' the third man said warningly.

'I think Doctor Eden should make sure for himself,' the Beard said flatly.

'Thank you,' Silk said, and looked at the woman admiringly. 'Your lady friend doesn't speak English.'

'She doesn't understand it. She can't speak. She's dumb.'

'Oh, poor girl. What's her name?'

'Wakhia.'

'Wakhia . . . Wakhia . . . delightful.'

She might be deaf too to judge from her expressionless stare. No sign of any reaction had come onto her face since the quartette had confronted him. He was sure it was the woman he had seen sitting on the boulder. For one thing her hair though thicker than he imagined last evening was uncovered and unbraided; that went against the run of his briefing about the women of Turikrun. The other details were what he had noticed: the brown ankle-length gown with flowing wide sleeves, the shapeless corsage with the large slack fold – which might be to cover anticipated pregnancy because the women here were too poor to have more than one gown – and fastened round her waist by a broad woollen belt like a cummerbund, several coils of silver wire necklets, others of brightly coloured plaited wools, a tall one round her neck held by upright oblong silver ornaments. She looked fearsomely healthy. He saw nothing likely to wilt.

'Poor woman,' he said, and glanced round. 'Will you lead the way?' he asked the Beard, smiling.

Throughout their silent stroll through the wood and up the

pass Silk found his mind divided into three main channels. First, a need to remain sufficiently in the rear to allow himself time to poise and try to do something if they changed their minds and came at him. Secondly, a wonder about why three obvious Britons, well-educated despite everything to give a contrary view to be gained from their appearance, came to be living in a valley where Bell had been the only white man until he sent his last message. That was the third thought in his mind. Priest had told him how long ago Bell had sent his last message but he had forgotten it, along with other small details which he usually had no trouble in recalling instantly.

Halfway up the short but steep pass, no more than a few hundred feet, the Kafir woman fell back from the men to being only a couple of paces ahead of him. He saw no reason for her action. Propinquity did not exactly titillate his male instincts: the length and folds of her gown gave her a nunlike quality. He had even seen nuns hurrying with the same impatient long stride along hot city pavements.

The answer to his question about her reason came almost accidentally. When they were some distance up the pass he glanced up at the sheer high ground rising straight up on either side of them.

Outlined against the ribbon of brilliant blue sky were three men in Western clothes, two on the left, one on the right. All of them were watching the small party on the pass. They did not move. Their stillness added another dimension of strangeness to the atmosphere. Not only because he saw that each man carried an automatic rifle.

5

The Valley of Turikrun presented a strange sight after the contrasts of wild empty countryside which led to it.

Silk halted. He saw no reason to be rushed headlong into the valley until he had some comprehension of its characteristics. He needed that in case events forced him to try to leave in a hurry.

On either side of the wide trail which dropped steeply into the valley were wide stretches of woodland patched with bushes. At a rough guess it was about three miles long, possibly more, and nearly a mile wide. There might well be another valley farther on. This one was bisected by a narrow winding river. A variety of trees, predominantly pines and larch, were in long wavy strips on various levels of the valley floor, flanking fields of corn, millet, and barley. Women in dark brown robes were at work in the fields and among mulberry bushes, apricot and walnut trees, or laying out fruit to ripen on the flat roofs of houses. Other women carried heavily-laden baskets on their backs as they toiled up short but steep rises of ground to clusters of log houses which formed the village; almost all the houses were at this end of the valley with only a few farther on. Beyond on the left side of the village a large sloping field of beans flanked a *mandao-jao*, 'place of many coffins'; the coffins were scattered haphazardly across the ground. Below the *mandao-jao* was a small solitary building which he took to be the *jestak-kan*, the village temple, and high above the *mandao-jao* was a sort of *ziarat*, a shrine, decorated with tattered flags, ibex horns, twisted of coloured paper. Both temple and shrine indicated a continuation of the religion once shared by these Black Kafirs with their Red Kafir cousins in Afghanistan.

Although there were women everywhere Silk saw few men. Those in sight at this hour were either old or had an obvious physical deformity or were slender *onjesta-mosh*, the teen-age boy virgins so highly regarded by Kafir tribespeople. Silk noted that the women wore . . .? what was the thing called? . . . ah! a *kupis* on their head, a dark brown coif decorated with a huge pom-pom of coffee-coloured wool surrounded by rows of cowrie shells which descended down the back with various metal buttons and silver or tin ornaments; several scholars had likened the *kupis* to a coif worn by women in ancient Greece. Overall the houses were substantially built, of long squared logs chinked with stones and mud. They appeared commodious and could be mistaken for pioneer log-cabins.

Silk felt some misgiving. It might be a very difficult place to leave in a hurry. There were a lot of people here. And such communities usually started work at sunrise.

He allowed himself one small inward cheer. So far the briefing he had done about this place and its people, even some words of the dialect they shared with other Kafir valley communities which had disappeared in recent years, had returned without much effort on his part. It augured well. He inclined to believe that the main holes in his memory were indeed limited to the period between when he emplaned at Cyprus and awoke with a frantic headache in the other valley.

He saw that the men and the woman had stopped some paces ahead and had turned to watch him. Their lack of speech since they approached the pass suggested they had taken a communal vow of silence. He glanced behind him. Four men, not three, all Caucasians, were coming down from their presumable look-out posts above the pass. All of them were armed.

He hurried forward. 'I'm so sorry to have delayed you all but what a place?' he exclaimed enthusiastically. 'What a beautiful place! The hills, those mountains, this marvellous air, such a picturesque valley – magnificent! Truly magnificent! An artist's delight!'

None of them spoke. They merely turned and walked on though the woman hovered until he almost reached her. Her face was no longer expressionless. For some reason she looked enormously proud. She gave him a long and lingering smile, the sort of smile a girl might give her lover. That was it! She looked possessive.

As they neared the village he saw that several of the nearest women were quite young. Among remote tribal peoples it was easy to detect the bloom of youth, easier than in lands where the mature used a variety of aids to imply youth and a larger percentage of the young looked old and anxious. Several of these women were triumphantly pregnant. Surely that was wrong? No, his eyes had not misled him.

He wondered if his memory had started to limp again. According to the very thorough briefing Priest had given him, Black Kafir women who were pregnant were shut up in a special house a? . . . a *bashali*, along with all still fruitful women who were incarcerated in a *bashali* for five or six days a month; both events in a woman's life here were regarded as 'times of defilement' and the *bashali* was their quarantine ward. The briefing had said that only a local midwife could enter a *bashali*; she had to go in completely naked and bath immediately she left, whatever the season or hour and before she dressed herself; he had said to Priest: 'Doesn't she have to gargle too?' Nothing in the briefing had said anything about Women's Lib raising its head here. Something had happened to break a quantity of sacred *tabus*. Bell must have tried to tell someone about it and failed to get through the jamming of his messages.

As in similar communities the virgin boys bore themselves like young Apollos. They looked pale and uninteresting and horribly pampered. Their transparent vanity was loathsome to behold. It could only mean that here they were more protected than all the débutantes who once caused traffic jams in London. The people provided another surprise.

They were said to be fair-skinned. Once you crossed the Iranian frontier into Afghanistan the description became suspect. Usually it meant a sort of unshiny coffee colour. But these people, the women, the little male virgins, the few older Turikrun men in sight, had genuinely fair complexions and were no darker than southern Italians or Greeks. Perhaps it was true that long ago a large quantity of Greeks were transported into this region.

'Wait here', the Beard ordered abruptly.

Silk thought it best to ask no questions yet. The Beard and his companions were obviously not in charge of anything; they lost their tempers too easily, always a sign of lack of authority, and this instruction proved it.

'Thank you,' he said politely.

He ignored the other members of the group and the small crowd of inquisitive tribespeople and the four armed men, and glanced round.

They had stopped several yards below one of the larger houses some five hundred yards from where the village street began. He watched the Beard stride quickly towards the house and vanish up a flight of narrow steps leading to living-quarters above the ground-floor space for storage and goats. 'Village' and 'street' were basically wrong descriptions. There was no street as such, just a broad ragged trail, caused by time, which went off down the valley. The houses were untidy dwellings, very solid, but constructed close together, appearing to rise in tiers as they climbed the steeply rising ground. He had an idea that originally they might have housed members of a family. He guessed that their pale wood was green Turkey oak and walnut.

The storage space under the family quarters was clearly designed for good crops and the narrow steps for protection from starving wild dogs in winter. As he had seen on the walk down from the head of the pass the flat roofs were filling up with fruit to ripen.

The circle of people around him were whispering. Several of the men had an intense emotional stare as if some wildness lurked just below the surface of their minds. They wore loose barracans or chalvers. Each man wore a Chitrali bonnet, a curious porridge-coloured circular woollen affair like a small tyre with a pancake of the same hue flat on the top. Only the boy virgins affected a supercilious disdain of a visitor in their midst.

After ten minutes or so Silk looked at Mr Hawkins and Mr Becket. 'What has happend to Mr Hawks?' he asked petulantly.

Neither of them answered. Becket gazed at his long fingers with the absorption of a medium in a trance. Hawkins shifted his weight from one leg to the other and back again.

Silk turned and repeated the question to the four armed men.

Three of them gazed at him moodily. The fourth responded with a sort of savage smile and his lips twitched. When he glanced at the woman he saw that her prideful mood had increased. She was busy looking at women in the surrounding crowd with the smile of someone who had just won a record sum on the football pools. She glanced at him with proprietorial fondness.

It seemed a moment to state a position. He turned his gaze back to Mr Hawkins and Mr Becket. They were still busy with their own thoughts.

'Now look here,' he said angrily. 'I appreciate you people dislike strangers who arrive unexpectedly. You've already made that perfectly clear. But my friend will be extremely annoyed when he hears about this. It is no way to treat a visitor.'

He had to chance to go on. Mr Hawkins took two steps forward and slapped him twice across the mouth. His hand was too softly plump to do more than sting. He too realized that immediately for he clenched it into a fist and took a swing at Silk's ear which would have inspired Mohammed Ali to write a poem. Seconds later Mr Hawkins sat up on the dusty path, shook his head, and gazed up at Silk with hot eyes. He scrambled to his unsteady feet.

'Grab him', Mr Hawkins said breathlessly.

Two of the armed men dropped their weapons and seized Silk's arms and dragged them back. Silk braced himself. He saw Mr Hawkins rush forward with the clear intention of working him over now that they were on what the man regarded as fair terms. The pudgy fists whirled like a gale-struck windmill. Their obvious destination was Silk's stomach. Whatever he lacked in strength he obviously intended to rectify by ferocity. Silk poised on his toes, using the gripping arms to steady his balance. His left foot caught Mr Hawkins under the chin. The man yelped and fell on his back. Mr Becket hastened forward.

'What the hell is going on?' shouted the voice of Mr Hawks.

Mr Becket stopped abruptly. 'This fool started to mix it with Francis,' he said savagely.

'That is an exaggeration,' Silk contradicted him, and gave his account of events as his arms were freed and Mr Hawkins crawled round on the ground and finally got to his feet.

'That sounds more logical.' The Beard sounded very amiable, full of charm. He turned to his unsteady friend. 'You're too impetuous, Francis,' he chided like a long-suffering nanny. He turned back to Silk. 'Francis gets terrible headaches, Doctor. Perhaps you could treat him.'

Silk stared at him indignantly. 'I am not that sort of doctor,' he replied shortly. At the same instant his gaze went to a point high up on the steep hillside above the nearest cluster of houses. Puzzled by what he saw there he looked coldly at the Beard; it was better to deal with first things first. 'I don't understand why I am being subjected to this treatment,' he said icily.

'I've come a long way to visit an old friend who invited me here.' He kept his voice high, in order to be overheard by anyone near who might understand basic English. 'You and these men greeted me with extreme hostility. Now your friend attacks me. These . . . these warders treat me like a criminal. I shall complain to my friend. Where is he?'

The hair hid any expression on Mr Hawks's face but he kept his voice mild. 'We're having some trouble in finding him', he said apologetically 'You probably know he's inclined to go for long walks without telling anyone.'

The man's whole attitude had changed since he went off to see whoever he had seen.

'Then why am I kept waiting here?' Silk demanded indignantly. 'Take me to his house. I'll wait there for him'.

Hawks looked uneasy. 'It may not be possible,' he said worriedly.

'Why? Don't be absurd!'

'It's not as simple as it might appear.'

'What is impossible about waiting at the home of a friend who invited you to visit him?'

'We think he may be away. On one of his walks into the hills.'

'Oh'?

Hawks gave the appearance of a man floundering in a situation with which he could not cope. 'Perhaps that's why I couldn't remember him at first,' he said lamely. 'We don't see much of him. He keeps to himself.'

Silk snorted. While he hesitated, frowning, trying to demonstrate that he was only partly appeased by the the explanation, he glanced up at the place on the hillside which he had noted earlier. He had not been mistaken. High up there were the broken remains of a bright green and dust-coloured helicopter. A faint echo of memory collected somewhere told him it was a German BO 105. Some navigational error or unexpected change of wind due to these hill formations must have caused it to belly-flop onto the hillside and break into three main sections. Two men in Western-style clothes were at work beside it. Memory tried to convince him that he had seen either that chopper or another like it. And so he must have done somewhere some time ago or why should he imagine he knew which sort of machine it was?

He saw the scene up there for only a split second lest it seemed that he was curious. Then he sighed and looked at Hawks again. A sixth sense warned him against pushing it too hard.

'Well, if we can't get into the house . . . ' he said aimlessly.

'Oh, I thought I said he always keeps it locked,' the other man interrupted hastily. 'He's rather a recluse, not like you.'

The others had gone silent. Only the girl seemed normal. She had a bright smile on her face. Her gaze never left Silk. It had a fond glint which missed no detail.

'Well, where do I go?' Silk asked testily. 'I've had a long walk. I'm tired and hungry.'

Hawks nodded sympathetically. 'I'll take you to Wakhia's house,' he said. 'She'll see you have some food and are comfortable. She had earned the right. Ferdy wants you to feel completely at home. He'll see you later. He's rather busy at present.'

'Who is Ferdy?' Silk asked as they walked on.

'Ferdy Fay? He's our leader. You'll love him. Everyone loves Ferdy. We're a community. We came here to escape from so-called civilization. Until your friend gets back Wakhia will attend to you.'

It sounded more than pat. It sounded very unusual. None of the men whom Silk had seen up till now resembled the one-time 'flower-people', harmless dropouts from the rat race who only wanted to be left alone to do their own thing. This lot had rat race faces. They also had rifles.

Silk shrugged. 'Very well,' he agreed irritably. 'Provided I'm not wasting the young woman's time.'

The other man laughed like a bark. 'You'll have to put up with her,' he said. 'As I told you, she has earned the right.

It's a custom here. Most of the local men have gone to work in the south, usually Karachi or over in Kabal. Wakhia was the first woman to see you. Ferdy'll tell you about the local customs when he sees you.'

Silk did not answer as they went on, followed by the armed men and a ragged crowd. His head had started to ache; reaction, he told himself. His legs felt weak and leaden alternately. Yes, events of the last hour or so were beginning to take their toll. Worse, he had many confusing new things to think about. He had to think about them now.

6

An hour later Silk began to feel less confused. Much of the heat had gone out of his head. He supposed it was a form of reaction or a natural consequence of getting a wallop on the computer without having on hand a choir of delicious nurses to improve the morale.

He had spent most of the time sitting on the balcony of the house to which they had brought him. The gloomy smoke-blackened and stale-smelling rooms, reached by the vertigo-nightmare outside steps of some eighteen inches high by about ten inches wide per step and without a handrail or guard, held no attraction for him. The heat inside them was so solid up against his nose that he felt it would be possible to cut out a chunk and carry it away. Out here in the shade and lesser heat, although he provided a sitting duck for anyone eager to prove himself a helluva marksman, the air had swept out some of the hugger-mugger in his head. And although the smell of goats which came from every side was pretty pungent it was not too bad; since he sat down he had seen that the goat population of Turikrun far outnumbered the human community. In his peripatetic years he had endured worse smells.

The armed guard posted at the base of the steps round the side of the house gave another dry cough. It provided the only proof that he was still there. Silk was not sure whether the man coughed from boredom or habit or just to let him know that he was under virtual house-arrest.

He knew that many things needed his urgent consideration but his mind merely droned like a lazy bee enjoying sunlight before search. It refused to see anything clearly. Events had fuzzed each other so completely that at present they resembled out-of-focus photographs, no single outline sharp. So, resentfully, guiltily, he just sat waiting for the spirit to activate him. He always felt guilty if he did not hurry around doing what he knew had to be done; his reputation in the old firm came from being a trouble-shooter, able to improvise and get on with the job. This laziness was bad, bad. It had never happened to him before. He hoped to God it would never happen again.

Without much urgency he looked at the valley and noted its life. Two things helped to increase his lotus-eating mood. The rough kitchen-type chair on which he sat had come as a welcome surprise in this region where most primitive peoples, and many others, did without such fads. It had taken him some while to recall that the Kafirs had long used them. And inside the house behind him the woman hurried about preparing a meal. He wondered precisely what Hawks meant when he said she had earned the right to him. Something told him St. Paul would not have approved.

Those were minor points. Only one positive factor led him to hope in fits and starts that his ability to think clearly would return soon even if his memory remained faulty; training insisted that he pay attention to his surroundings and get them crystal-clear in his mind. Every agent had to decide which were the most important elements in any situation. Here, somewhat restricted in brain and defence, the most important element appeared to be place, in case he had to run for it. He had told Hawks that friends of his would arrive to pick him up. When he met this man Ferdy he could build that out to a couple of days, maybe three. That should keep him fairly safe for roughly fortyeight hours, provided nothing happened to arouse their suspicions. To his numb mind two or three days did not seem much.

His attempts to think were interrupted as the woman came out of the room behind him and put a tentative hand on his shoulder. He feigned ignorance of the contact. After a few moments she went back into the house. None of this fitted into the briefing given him by Priest.

He went back to memorizing the landscape.

From this balcony the roofs of other houses blocked out sections of the valley. None of the houses had been laid out in trim relation to each other; they were jammed tightly together at varying angles and separated only by narrow alleys. Above the top of the opposite hillside a long range of permanent snowcaps rose into the sunlight. They were shaped like partly eaten ice-cream in cones; he thought they must be part of the Hindu Kush, the 'Killer of Hindus' who had been unable to endure its bitter cold and perilous ascents, though they might be part of Karakoram; no, Karakoram was too far north. He sketched it out in his mind to be doubly sure.

Deep jagged clefts like giant claw-marks scarred the top of the hillside. Beneath each was a spill of talus. Some were decorated with clumps of tall grass resembling feather head-dresses, probably the result of airborne spores. Between the falls of scree he saw a few arthritic cypresses, old and misshapen as Macbeth's witches. Narrow trails worn by goats and streams wound down amid rock obstructions and vanished into pine and larch copses, emerged briefly and disappeared again in the lower, heavily wooded slopes. He was given a slight sign that a section of memory had begun to work; he recognised the trees lower down as deciduous, and they were fringed by walnuts, planes, mulberries and willows. From some streams higher up appeared busy and wider rivulets which merged into the glittery river which broadened along the floor of the valley.

One long look at the hillside convinced him that it provided no easy escape route. He had known harder roads. But this one presented endless problems. Even if he reached the top, a highly controversial matter, the achievement would give no guarantee of success. It would be the commencement of a long walk across hostile country in a thin atmosphere to – where? sustained by what? facing what sort of dangers? If he went back in the direction from which he had come here these men could follow him. If he went southeast it would take him to Afganistan. Either way there would pose endless hardships.

His only good chance lay in going back by the way he reached here. Whatever the risks.

In fortyeight hours' time.

Less if he could do all that he had to do.

He turned his attention to the people who appeared from or vanished into the houses. On the way here Hawks had told him that nearly ninety per cent of able-bodied Turikrun men had overcome their historic distaste for work and gone to seek their fortunes in southern Pakistan or Afghanistan. Some had gone to India, claiming that as Turikrunis they were neither Pakistanis or Afghans and religious wars meant nothing to them because they were neither Muslim nor Hindu. None, Hawk said, had returned. They had abandoned their wives, their families, their small children. None could write home; they were illiterate. According to Hawks, the remaining men intended to follow their friends.

The majority of those Silk could see had positive 'Alpine' characteristics. Many had blue eyes and only a few had really black hair. None had the heavy Mongoloid eyefold. Only a very few were swarthy and had a deeper pigmentation round the eyes. None of them wore shoes; they were either barefoot or had strips of rag wound round their insteps and ankles which were held by leather thongs. They slouched about, without noticeable purpose or routine. Most of them had a shifty air. He would not trust them in his sight or behind his back on a lonely path in full daylight.

The few small children in sight were undernourished little things. One and all looked heir to every childish and most other ailments. The little girls were noticeably more lively than their brothers.

These outward signs of a decaying remote community were strange because the brown-robed and multi-pigtailed women were vastly different.

At first sight any strangers might have been misled by their demure robes into thinking they were a community of Asian-style nuns. He would not have thought so for long. Silk could not recall having seen women so transparently proud and confident of their sexuality. One glance told you that the robes were a conventional attire any one of them would have got rid of if anybody suggested it. Each one might have been a queen, her pom-pom and cowrie-decorated *kupis* a crown symbolic of vitality and purpose. They were taller than most women in adjoining countries. The skins of some were so pale that they were creamy. If his memory was right no Kafir woman had ever worn the veil or the Afghan *chaddar*. Even older women with greying hair and lined faces had a spritely vigour unmatched by any man who had managed to reach their age. Some of the women between fifteen and thirtyfive had adopted the practice of Chitrali women of rimming their eyelids with kohl. A few had big black tribal marks smeared across their foreheads. They exuded assurance. This alone separated them from most Asian women whose meekness was habit become custom, at least in public. They were gorgeous and quite frightening.

So much for the Kalash, or Kafir, people of the village forgotten by big nations engaged on the important tasks of proving their historic destiny by intriguing and fighting to become Number One in the region.

Somewhere across the valley a rifle cracked dully.

The noise sounded as if it came from high up.

When Silk looked at the general region from which the sound came his searching gaze saw nothing at first. Then on one sunlit strip of ground hundreds of feet below a path of sheer wall-like cliff which soared directly to the summit he saw a tiny antlike figure stumbling and scrambling from left to right across a strip of pebble-sized talus. Instinct told him the ant was a man. The man found the going hard. Frequently his feet seemed to sink ankle-deep into the talus, impeding his progress and making him stagger and throw up tiny arms to keep his balance. Each time he managed to keep going. Silk got an impression that between moments when the man flung up his arms he seemed to be holding his right side between the ribs and hip. At this distance he appeared to be wearing a dark shirt and trousers. It was impossible to guess his true intention but his actions and the shot suggested he was trying to escape from something, evidently to reach some point which he believed likely to give him a degree of safety. On and on his tiny antlike figure went, scrambling and leaping and stumbling towards a point where a fold of hillside was swallowed in shadow. Once he slid several feet down in the talus but managed to keep his balance. Another report reached the village. The distant man seemed to be tiring. Suddenly he stopped, only yards from the long wavy fold of shadow. At this distance it seemed as if something must have jarred his head back on his neck and his arms spread out in front of him. The dull sound of several reports followed each other in swift succession. The man pitched forward onto his knees, got up laboriously and stood still, and then pitched forward onto his face. This time he did not get up.

A quick glance showed Silk that everyone he could see down here in the village had stopped to watch whatever drama was taking place on the other side of the valley. Even the boy virgins had reverted to being ordinary spectators.

Silk corrected himself. All except one. The armed guard who Hawks had stationed at the foot of the precipitate steps, ostensibly to ensure that no one disturbed his rest with excessive neighbourliness and let Wakhia look after him, had emerged into sight. For some reason, he had turned to see if Silk was watching what happened on the other hillside.

Instinctively Silk stretched his arms lazily and opened and shut his mouth a couple of times like a man testing his tongue after being awakened from a doze. His deep yawns required no acting. He blinked and stretched. Two other men had come into view on the sunlit patch, walking cautiously forward across the talus towards the fallen man. Silk rubbed the back of his neck, turning his head stiffly from side to side. The men reached the man who had fallen and stopped; then they turned towards the village, raising their arms as if in jubilation. In one hand each of them held a rifle. Momentarily they resembled figures in one of those fading photographs of victorious warriors of either side in the Boer War.

Silk became aware of someone standing beside him. He looked up and saw it was Wakhia. The smile she gave in response to his greeting was radiant though a bit nervous. He got to his feet and turned his back to the watchful eyes below and went through the motions of giving the woman a friendly embrace though in fact he only took hold of her elbows to keep her there while he thought. A sort of vibration rather than a shiver went through her at the same moment but she appeared to enjoy the meaningless contact.

'Good!' he exclaimed heartily, and yawned. 'Excuse me. This air is very tiring. I must have dozed off.' He spoke loudly enough to be heard by the guard below and made a pantomime snoring noise. 'Sleep, you know?'

As he spoke he slid his hands up to her shoulders and his finger-tips touched her bare neck. He hoped the action might produce some visible indication of pleasure; some people, particularly women of her age, communicated their moods far more clearly by sigh or smile than by use of pebbly words. His action did far more. She gave a grateful sough of pleasure, true enough, but her smile was stiff as a railway line and she trembled violently. Her face had the blank expression of a heavy-weight boxer about not to hear the count of ten. He had a belittling conviction that none of it had much to do with him.

Nonetheless, it gave him the chance to spread thoughts through being overheard by the guard.

'God, you beautiful wild creature!' he exclaimed in his best gone voice. 'So young too. A wild lovely child.' He sounded as impressible as James Bond.

The woman clearly understood the tone of his voice even if the words were unknown. A tremulous uncertainty replaced the stiff expression and fastened her attention on him. It was a shame to use her like this and he disliked himself for it. But he had to play everything on the ear and he was sure that Hawks had posted a guard who understood English without trouble. It would pay him to have the guard report back that he was in a completely relaxed mood, uncurious about anything except the woman. It also gave him a chance to think about the scene he had just witnessed.

So he let his thumb communicate his pleasure in the firm smooth skin of her cheek and then let his hands wander over her gown. Under it she was clearly a fine strapping wench. The opinion spread by a few foreigners who had reported their contacts with the Kafirs and generally found them to be filthy did not apply to this woman; she smelled of sunshine and summery dust and cold mountain stream water. While he held her there so that the guard could see them if he stepped back a couple of paces she closed her eyes and submitted.

After a moment he gave a little excited laugh which sounded like a lick over future prospects. The woman opened her eyes and smiled at him, an easier smile, positive communication. She had stopped trembling. He put an arm round her waist and turned.

The guard below lowered his watchful eyes and turned aside. He paced off round the house out of sight. People out in the village had resumed their walk to wherever they were going. Off on the distant hillside two ants were carrying the third between them as they descended a narrow track towards a strip of woodland.

He kept smiling at the woman though his mind had slipped back towards confusion once again. It felt hot and troubled. So many things needed to be thought about, clearly, coolly, without haste or tension. These people here, not the villagers for whom he had been prepared but the guards, these Europeans, males, young men of the activist revolutionary years. That helicopter smashed up on the hillside behind the village. The man injured or dead, probably dead, on the other hillside, the man whose identity he thought he could guess. Other things. He felt as if he were sliding into a trance of confusion and dragged himself back to the immediate surroundings and the woman looking up at him with a smile on her face.

'Food,' he said and made an eating motion with his mouth.

His companion nodded. She shaped her lips as if to speak the word, a frown of intense concentration on her forehead, then she smiled wryly and seemed to wait for him to speak. When he did not do so her strong clasp drew him back from the balcony into the hot dark room. It had never ceased to surprise him how any woman could shed an outward show of weak indulgence and become intensely pragmatic about household affairs faster than an ambitious politician could switch from vilifying his opponents to proclaim himself more highminded than an archangel. As his eyes grew accustomed to the gloom he saw that she had been busy while he sat outside. She had tidied the room, a wide square with a minimum of furniture and none of the knick-knackeries which other peoples thought proof of civilisation, and had prepared them a meal of fresh white mulberries, eggs, and thin flat wheatbread fried to crispness in ... clarified butter ... was it *ghi*? didn't you need buffalo-milk to make *ghi*? He had forgotten. It did not matter at present except that it provided additional proof of his stuttering memory. There were also apricots and a great mound of outside walnuts and – oh luxury! – an enamel pot and cups of tea.

'Marvellous!' he exclaimed and hoped she understood his gratitude from his tone.

She fetched the chair from the balcony and placed it alongside him at the rickety table.

While the light faded outside their meal took on a sort of Chelsea or Greenwich Village or Left Bank atmosphere. They might have been young lovers – if young lovers could afford to live in those property speculators' Meccas – for she insisted on tasting everything before he ate it. As she did so her face reverted to the enigmatic expression he had seen on it earlier, her blank eyes demanding his attention. Somewhere or other – either in one of Margaret Mead's studies of primitive people or Malinovski's work on *Sex and Repression in Savage Society* – he had read that the women of some remote tribes believed that if a woman ate food from the dish of, and drank from the same cup as, the man she desired her body would be more receptive to his seed. Every people had its cherished gooseberry bush superstitions. Especially those facing extinction. He wondered if he could avoid paying the price of accepting her companionship without awaking a fury worse than that of hell.

Their inability to gossip about the weather or local scandals gave him another chance to think. She scarcely moved, her gaze concerned only with his face. Occasionally she smiled unsurely at him.

He could have made good use of a drink. Foremost amongst the things which needed his attention was the significance of what he had witnessed taking place on the opposite hillside. Another question partly overlay that event. Belatedly he had realised that he was conscious of Wakhia standing beside him for some time before he acknowledged her presence. So she must have seen at least part of what happened. Yet when he stood up and the guard's curiosity attracted his attention and forced him to pretend he had not seen anything, her face had been expressionless even though people abroad in the village had stopped to watch the incident. Her control over her face was faultless; he had already noted that it showed precisely what she wanted it to show. Now that the guard had gone her face mirrored his own moods.

Through the gathering darkness he studied her with new interest. Her gaze met his steadily. Her pale eyes seemed to offer trust; or was it something he failed to define? Something more stable than the 'imprint look' due to sexual attraction? It certainly had a masked tension outside the range of attraction.

None of his experiences amongst and reading of remote communities helped him to define whatever her eyes attempted to convey. If there was anything at all. He could not be sure.

About an hour after the woman had lit an ancient oil-lamp they had visitors. They had been sitting in the pale quarter-light busy with their separate thoughts when there was an exchange of voices below followed by footsteps climbing towards them. For a moment he was caught unprepared and felt apprehensive; then he knew it must be Hawks and the man he called Ferdy. That reassured him somewhat though it did not lessen his apprehension; these men were fighting fit, but of energy and a total memory, unlikely to betray them or cause them to panic.

The woman looked at him nervously as they heard an authoritative knock on the door. He braced himself and smiled confidently. His feet ached as he stood up and she went to answer.

7

Oliver Hawks marched into the room past the silent woman. In the pale light and surrounded by smoke-blackened walls he could scarcely be seen; his fashionable Neanderthal wealth of hair made him almost invisible. His nose and eyes seemed to float forward across the room. Neither Mr Hawkins the Tub nor Mr Becket the Dude Peon was with him.

The man who did follow him created a vastly different atmosphere. Silk was positive he had not seen him until now. The man was all of six feet four tall, so tall indeed that he had to bend his head and shoulders forward to prevent leaving them outside as he entered. When he straightened up Silk saw he was thin to the point emaciation. Unlike other European types here in the valley he did little to win contemporary approval by his appearance. By present standards his dark hair was short; it was neatly part on the left side and two tidy wings looped back above his well-formed ears. His face was thin, pale down to its careful brown moustache and curly sparse beard. He had a carefully tended old brown linen safari jacket with patch breast pockets and belted over an open-necked lilac-toned shirt; his flannel trousers were also ancient and carefully preserved. The long brown leather sandals revealed long pale toes. His age might be anything from thirtyseven to fortyfive and was wholly insignificant. He gazed at Silk with gentle, tragic eyes. Only a plastic crown of thorns was missing. He was like a well-tended grave.

'This,' Hawks said reverently, 'is Ferdy'. He dithered aside like a nervous chaplain ushering in an archbishop. 'Our leader.'

'Peace be with you, Doctor Eden,' Ferdy said. He had a soft caressive voice reminiscent of those genteel anonymities who sell anything from bras to cheese on British television adverts. 'I hope Sister Wakhia has made you comfortable after your long walk. She is a warm and loving soul.'

'Everything has been excellent, Mr Fay.'

The man raised a gentle hand. Its long tapering fingers were so smooth they appeared boneless. The action was done positively as if he were about to deliver a blessing. 'Call me Ferdy,' he said with a sad smile. 'Everyone in our community does, and you are our honoured guest. We are humble to welcome you into our midst.'

'Thank you, Ferdy.' Silk said, and did his best to appear at his own impressible best. He knew he would fail. He never felt homey about fake gurus and crystal-gazers and that bunch. 'Yes, Sister Wakhia has been most helpful. Since those men misunderstood my irritation.'

Ferdy dismissed the incident with a slow wave of his hand. 'Some of our newer brethren are not yet familiar with our path in humility,' he said contritely, 'It is our rule that when a guest arrives I should be told immediately even if I am at contemplation. I have reprimanded our brothers. They will apologize to you. They are very sensitive and alarmed in case our community, its peace here away from the brutal world which has persecuted us, is destroyed by evil forces. I am sorry that your arrival here was so unfortunate.'

Silk realized that he was not the only one peculiar in the head though he had the advantage of knowing it. 'I understand their vigilance,' he said cheerfully. 'Peace is a beautiful thing to possess.'

'Ah! I knew you understood our attitude. Peace of mind is sacred. Did the other disturbance upset you?'

'Was there one?' Silk queried, wide of ingenuous eye. He

gave a short, apologetic laugh. 'Directly Wakhia found me a chair I sat out on the balcony and fell asleep. It must be the mountain air. And the exercise, of course. It took Wakhia, ah forgive me, Sister Wakhia several minutes to wake me up for the meal she had prepared while I took it easy.' He tchtched in annoyance. 'Ferdy, my manners are atrocious. Please sit down. And you, Brother Oliver.'

Ferdy smiled. 'I prefer to stand,' he announced as if laying down an article of faith. 'You must rest to regain strength for your return journey.' It sounded like a special dispensation.

Silk sat down again. 'What happened?' he asked interestedly.

Ferdy gestured vaguely. 'The incident was of no importance,' he said in the same sad, remote tone. 'You have seen how our friends, the poor natives here, accept us and our mission joyously. Some have found great fulfilment in our message.'

'I expect they associate you with their historic past.'

'You know about that?'

'Alexander the Great and the march of his legion nearby if not actually in this valley,' Silk said, and added a few details to harden his alibi.

Ferdy nodded. 'Exactly exactly,' he agreed. 'Unfortunately, some misguided people in two other valleys seek to harm us and prevent our truth from being spread among the people. That was why my brothers misunderstood your reason for coming here.' His voice had taken on a deep sonorous quality; he seemed to be listening to every word. He shook his head regretfully. 'While you slept some of our vigilant brothers had to chase away one man from another valley who threatened our harmony of mind and freedom to contemplate.'

Silk gazed up at the other man full of admiration. It wasn't a case of saying that Ferdy should have been an actor. He was one. Every sentence he spoke had genuine authority, utter conviction in what he said as he said it. He would have been a fine Shakespearian actor, completely at home as Hamlet or Laertes or Hamlet's father or Macbeth or Iago, a score of roles which Silk had seen performed with far less sincerity than Ferdy put into his part as leader of a small group of modern-style religious drop-outs eager to be rid of the wear and tear of combative industrial politics. Silk did not believe in the act for an instant but he admired Ferdy's skill.

On one point Silk admitted himself beaten. Ferdy did not use the slovenly English favoured by most indigenous gurus. He spoke precisely, searching for the apt word and giving it stress. Another thing was his accent. It was not English though many people might have accepted it as such. It had a sort of sibilance, nothing sharply noticeable or obvious, but an intona-tion. Usually Silk had no trouble in placing an accent directly he heard it. It came as an unpleasant shock to realize that this might be one of the subtleties of memory which had vanished down a hole in his mind.

'How right you are to safeguard your peace here!' he agreed heartily. 'You and your brothers.' He half-smiled and half-frowned. 'Naturally, as an archaeologist, I hope you won't destroy whatever remains of the local people's religions and customs. As the Afghans did in Red Kafir valleys in um mmmm was it eighteen-eightyfive?'

'Are you interested in religion, Doctor?'

'Religions would be more correct. People who do my work are usually absorbed by the faiths and customs of the communi-ties they study.'

'Do you specialise in any particular branch of archaeology?'

Silk gave the bright laugh of the middleaged student. 'No no, just the general subject,' he said. 'I may specialize later on.'

'It must be fascinating work.'

'It is. Naturally it does not appeal to many. But I have been fortunate in creating a wide television audience which appears to enjoy my programmes. In Britain and the Commonwealth. America too, of course. And some European countries where it is still a novelty.'

Ferdy smiled sadly. 'Is that why you came here?' he asked.

77

'Partly yes. As I told brother Oliver my old friend Bell invited me here to see what he thought were traces of the presence of Alexander the Great and his legion. I am sure he was right. It has been a long-standing invitation. In his last letter my friend told me he would be leaving here in a year or so. Fortunately I was quite near, working on a dig from which I could get here without much bother.'

'Near, you say?'

'Yes. In Turkey.'

'How fascinating. Tell me about it.'

Silk gave him the full treatment. He plunged in with details about marble and earthquakes, battered heads of deities, reconstructed basilicas, rare ornamentations likely to create a furore in the classical world, the vomitorium and ancient mosaics. He prattled on and on.

To do Ferdy justice, he never blinked an eye. That alone established him as a formidable character; individuals less used to the vocational chat they had sought in order to prove an individual's acceptability usually soon displayed signs of boredom and irritation. Ferdy listened. Without knowing a genuine thing about archaeology, he asked a string of careful questions which showed that he listened and adapted himself to whoever was talking to him, adroit as a woman in appearing to have a knowledge and interest in a subject far greater than she possessed in order to present a good social front. Silk chattered on, grateful for having some experience of what they discussed. Finally Ferdy ended the discussion with a gentle nod.

He gestured vaguely. 'I'm afraid we don't know what has happened to your friend,' he said worriedly. 'Did he expect you to arrive today?'

Silk frowned in order to give himself time to think. The man's slight accent still defeated his attempts to place it. He was conscious of Hawks shifting his weight occasionally from one foot to the other in the manner of a man unused to keeping still. Several paces farther off the woman was motionless as a statute, her face hidden by shadow.

'Well, he should have had my letter,' Silk said at length. 'I sent it at least eight or nine days ago.'

'Where did you send it from?'

'Turkey.'

'The place where you were digging.'

'Yes.'

'What did you say it was called?'

'Astartium.'

'Oh, yes. Is it near a large city?'

'It's quite new as a dig but not far from Ankara.'

'That is a main route airfield.'

Silk frowned thoughtfully again. 'I think so.' He gave another eldritch giggle. 'I'm never too sure about air-routes and things. They're hideously complicated.'

Ferdy gave an indulgent laugh. 'I think it would take three weeks, probably longer, for your letter to reach Chitral, Doctor Eden,' he said.

'Oh. Really?'

'I think so. Mr Bell did not go to Chitral last week.'

'Oh. Oh dear, oh dear.'

'Sometimes one of our brothers goes to see if he is in good health but he prefers not to join our community. At first we thought he resented our coming here. But that is only his manner. He is our friend.'

'He has lived alone for a long time.'

'Yes? We never ask anyone about their past life. Our concern is their future fulfilment in contemplation and meditation after we have ensured they are reborn.'

'I met a community like yours in Nepal,' Silk said thoughtfully. 'Very interesting. Wonderful people.'

'Ah, we left Nepal because too many people go there for spiritual salvation and are misled by false *gurus*.'

'Quite so. I saw some of them.'

Silk let it be seen that his thoughts were not concerned with Nepal. 'I don't know quite what to do,' he said worriedly.

'Your friend never told us when he intended to go up into the mountains. Only when he was going to Chitral, in case he could buy anything we needed, medical supplies though most of us now believe in spiritual healing. We did the same for him. Do you intend to wait for him? There seems to be no point if he is going to be away for two or three weeks.'

Silk resented being shoved. Nevertheless, this time he had only himself to blame for having given Ferdy the impression that he was a loon. He ignored the insult which caused Hawks to shift from one foot to the other and back again to prevent himself from laughing aloud. He shook his head unsurely.

'I expected this would be only a short trip because I warned him to be here,' he said. 'As I told Brother Oliver and his friends, my friends will pick me up in two or three days in their helicopter. That was the arrangement I made with them when they put me down so that I could walk here to see if I could recognize this as an area where Alexander and his legion came. I'm sure he must have expected me. Ah! Perhaps he left a letter for me at his house. I'd like to see it in the morning. It's a bit late to go there now.'

Ferdy hesitated. 'I don't quite know what to do.' he said finally. 'I would dislike it if he thought we broke into his house without permission and – forgive me, Doctor Eden – we have only your word that he is expecting you.'

'I assure you he is! We are very old friends!'

'I am sure you are,' Ferdy agreed soothingly. 'It is such a pity your letter did not reach him.' He paused uncertainly, Then, in the manner of a man not too sure if he was breaking a confidence, he went on: 'I think he sometimes visits a woman friend in another valley.' He laughed softly, as if amused by the follies of human nature. 'Our native sisters here have a problem of their nature, as Brother Oliver may have told you. Most of the men have gone away and left them behind. They are simple, warm-hearted souls. They have no wish to form an atttachment with Pakistanis or Afghans. Several of our brothers and disciples have formed liasions with them. It is unnatural for men and woman to live apart if they feel a need to indulge their heterosexual instincts. Our sisters here are drawn to my followers because of their fair skins and the colour of their hair and eyes. You will have observed the women here are like Sister Wakhia, Doctor Eden.'

'Yes yes yes, I was fascinated. It does appear to prove my theory. Consequently I was looking forward to spending at least two days here to collect enough information on their origin to provide a television programme in my series next year or the year after.'

Ferdy had walked into that threat to his plan to persuade the unwelcome guest to depart. He launched into a side issue to give himself time to think; Silk recognized the signs. 'The women have dreaded the loss of racial identity,' he stated sadly. 'Some have already vanished, abducted by Muslims for use as concubines or to become Karachi whores. You have seen that they are handsome women in youth. It is a penalty of the capitalist theory in most societies that women have their value judged solely on their appeal as sexual vessels. A few women committed suicide before we came, overcome by the torment of their problems. Now, surrounded by our brothers and disciples, they envelop us with love and gratitude. You have seen their joyous faces. I have seldom seen such love and devotion since my mission on earth began.'

Silk felt a need to vomit. It was real heady stuff. He wondered if he was expected to foam at the lips or get a glazed eye. It would be difficult; no nightclub stripper or soiled dove in a snassy flat, not even the bouncing bosoms of Las Vegas, had reduced him to age fifteen again.

'I see, I see,' he said in his doctorate voice. 'Excellent, excellent. They must feel themselves saved from great disaster.

No wonder they are grateful for having their problems solved by acceptance into the ranks of your followers.'

Ferdy gave a gratified smile.

'Could you enlighten me on one point?' Silk asked. 'When I arrived here, one of your brothers, I'm not sure which one, told me that Wakhia would provide me with comfort and companionship because she had earned the right by being the first woman here to see me. What did that mean?'

Ferdy nodded patiently. 'Since we began to arrive here a number of new believers from other places have come to join us,' he explained. 'Our unattached sisters here have devized a little competition among themselves. They try to be first to discover the next to join us. Wakhia was first to see you and mistook you for one of us.'

'One of your brothers.'

'Yes. While you are here she will attend to your needs.'

'I am grateful to her.'

'I will arrange for you to visit Mr Bell's house tomorrow to see if he left you a message,' Ferdy said. 'Tomorrow afternoon I will arrange for the local shaman to walk on live flames and for the boy virgins to entertain you. You know about the boy virgins? ... I thought you would have heard from Mr Bell. Later we will get the women to dance for you. They enjoy dancing. You may be able to tell us if the dance is Greek. Then you will be ready to leave with your friends if Mr Bell does not return. When will your friends be coming?'

'We left it rather open as to the hour,' Silk said. 'Either before dark the day after tomorow or some time during the next day. You are very kind to give me such hospitality when you are busy with your community affairs.'

Ferdy gave him a smile of ineffable sweetness and his long right arm rose towards the ceiling. It paused halfway up, rather like the old German Nazi salute. 'Peace be with you in your rest,' he said. He turned to the woman, his arm still partly raised. 'Peace and the fulfilment of your desire, little sister of the hills,' he said, and was gone.

Hawks followed him out silently.

Silk lowered his head and massaged the back of his neck. His headache had restarted abruptly; perhaps he only became aware of it now. The encounter had given him a strong feeling of nausea. Bogus religions and their adherents, the fashionable affluent which twittered their weird ideas like brainless sparrows always upset his digestion. But there was a big difference between most of them and this mob. Ferdy's brothers and disciples carried and used guns.

He sat still massaging his neck until the sound of footsteps faded away and the night was silent again. That meant people outside could hear what he said if he spoke too loudly and they were near. After a moment he raised his head and wiped a forefinger along the base of his nose. He glanced at the girl and would have sworn he saw the tinge of a smile on her shadowy face.

'Little sister of the hills', he said reflectively. Then he added: 'Well, leaving your desires aside, let's to bed, sister.'

8

They shared a bed in the spartan room reached through an open doorway from the other room and at the back of the house. Many things prevented him from achieving anything which approached true sleep. Real or imaginary, he kept hearing whispered exchanges between men at the foot of the steps outside; he thought it likely that Oliver Hawks had posted at least two men on guard there to prevent the honoured guest of Ferdy and his brotherhood from nosing about the village in search of something none of the brothers and disciples wanted him to find. Their hospitality was a thin veneer and lacked any substance or reality.

While he lay still questions tramped through his mind like the greatest migration of animals in history. None of them trailed an answer behind them. Each was an imponderable at present. Sometimes he almost fell asleep, worn out by the walk followed by the tensions produced by the various strangenesses he had already found here. Nevertheless, another part of his mind remained bright as an electric bulb. It reminded him in unfriendly fashion that his head still ached more furiously than a professional tennis-player's ego.

The bed was no remarkable aid. How it got here might be a secret epic of nineteenth-century progress. It had probably been sent from England to ensure the rest of a British army wife and might have come here via a forgotten missionary or early travel agent seeking to amaze the early customers of Thomas Cook &

Sons. Since those far-off youthful days many heavy men and women had robbed its springs of vitality. Perched on the edge, every time he neared anything approaching sleep he lost his balance and rolled down a slope steep as the Cresta Run at an ever-increasing speed. Somehow his companion managed to keep her balance on the other side of the abyss. He envied her sense of balance. Sometimes he resolved to remain fully awake in order that they should not be taken by surprise if Ferdy or one of his disciples changed his mind. At other times his mind swung lazily in the lunatic fringe between weary sleep and wearier consciousness.

At some time his senses reeled back through the clinging mud of mental confusion to slow realization that something had disturbed him.

It had also disturbed the woman. She had reacted faster. Light from the lamp she had carried when they entered the room showed her running to the doorway. Sensibly, much more sensibly than himself, she had taken off her clothes at some time unknown to him, to let her skin breathe in the stuffy room. He saw a mature female silhouette hastening away from him.

As he sat up stretching his arms he heard excited voices outside. They belonged mostly to women and shrill youths though he detected a few deeper masculine tones. They seemed to flick about like someone showing off their expertise with a pack of cards. It took him several frowning seconds to realize that the strangeness came from voices rising and fading as their owners raced past a huddle of houses which partially masked the sound. He gathered an impression that the people were heading away down the valley.

Wearily, he heaved himself off the bed and stumbled through the doorway. Wakhia was out on the balcony. A faint though sharp orange gleam illuminated the left side of her silhouette. It shone in her eyes too as she turned her head and looked up, aware of him joining her. She had left the lamp in the front room. Her hand fumbled for his and clutched it tightly.

The burning house which attracted such interest was a short distance down the valley. It was burning like a torch. Its own baleful light and that of stars illuminating the village showed that it stood by itself. He had not paid any particular attention to it earlier; he had paid no particular attention to any of them. As the flames took stronger hold they shot forty or more feet into the sky and licked out of its window-spaces, busy as village tongues at a gossip session. No current of air quickened the fire yet it burned as fiercely as if a gale were blowing. That suggested to him that it had been assisted.

While they stood watching it seemed as if half the village, possibly more, had risen from its beds to dash out to witness the event.

To judge from the excitement in the shouting voices every-one found the event most enthralling. Silk found that odd. True enough, in this age otherwise sane individuals – well, presumably sane – would drive fifty or a hundred miles to look at the remains of a crashed plane and see if bits of bodies were still being taken from the wreckage; they regarded it as a legitimate form of entertainment and sometimes took sandwiches and a flask of coffee to brace themselves against the shock. Yet, no, he would not have thought that these villagers would pay such attention to a burning house. Not unless the fact of its burning or its burning at this time or in this way seemed strange to them.

He freed his hand from the woman's nervous clasp and took two paces forward to peer over the balcony railing while he listened.

It did not take long for him to decide that two, possibly three, guards were on duty at the foot of the steps. They were out of sight from here. But he imagined that he heard one voicing some impatience to go and see the fire from closer quarters. One of them used words which should cause Ferdy to faint.

He went back to the woman and felt her hand clutch his tightly.

While they stood well back in the shadows the blaze continued without loss of vigour. Most fires did, large or small, until they had consumed whatever fed them. He wished he had some excuse to get down to the house without attracting attention to find out what fed this fire and caused it to burn so fiercely. Fires happened everywhere. There was always a cause. Without positive evidence, no one could say if this one had been started deliberately. It might have been put on, like a firework display, for his benefit. If it had, then either the house belonged to Bell or he was supposed to think it belonged to Bell. If the man on the hillside who had been shot and presumably killed was Bell, then it might well be Bell's. Why set fire to a disused house when your purpose was to destroy any possibility that the owner of a used house had left behind messages or evidence for someone to find? The someone being himself.

He corrected his foggy brain on a detail. The purpose of setting fire to an empty house, presuming that Bell was dead, could be to lead him into believing it was Bell's house on the off chance that he would go away, which would provide Ferdy and the brothers with a chance to search Bell's house minutely. For what? What did they expect or fear to find in it?

His brain packed up on him.

Another problem slithered into his thoughts. Something had awakened him. What? These rapid voices he heard now? An explosion? A twang of geriatric bedsprings as the woman left him to hasten here?

While they stood watching the flames two more armed brothers tramped up between the houses talking loudly enough to awaken everyone within earshot. At the foot of the steps they had a whispered conversation with the guards already down there, then all of them began to talk loudly. In German, with Bavarian accents. For a moment they went silent, then two of them talked louder on this side of the house and close to the balcony.

Silk read the message clearly. He freed his hand again and went forward to where the guards could see him clearly in the orange glow. He coughed twice as if afflicted by a dry throat, yawned noisily, and coughed again. There was no need to look down; they would know he was here, watching. The men continued to talk but lowered their voices.

He stayed in full sight until the fire started to die down. Only when the flames sagged and lost venom did he turn back to his companion. She looked most attractive wearing a simple little thing in moonlight and with a sliver of his shadow which did nothing to spoil the view. Ever since he romped around Paris and Venice with an excess of zeal and no talent as an art student his eyes had enjoyed the sight of a harmoniously proportioned woman whose vital areas provided a good female completeness. He thought she was a satisfying sight, a strong usable adequate woman well equipped for living. What he saw pleased him.

Although her head was partly hidden by his shadow he felt pretty sure her attention had switched from the dying blaze to himself.

By his reckoning they were at a mutual disadvantage. He had no reason to accept the story that she was voiceless. And if she had indeed earned the right to him, whatever the right involved, so far he had done little to give her cause to be pleased with her captive: himself. And, again from his viewpoint, if she had indeed been planted on him, because Bell had been 'persuaded' to tell Ferdy that he was coming here, it could only be to gain his confidence. He rejected that theory born of a tired mind at once: no one would use a voiceless woman for such a purpose. But there was another possibility. Most of these remote tribes had scores of tabus over a wide range of activities, most concerning conduct and behaviour. White men

88

frequently gave offence, often with dire results, quite unintentionally. Ferdy and his brothers might be trying to trick him into some error which have the genuine villagers thirsting for his blood within minutes or hours.

His headache had restarted, bothered by confusions and queries tumbling through it.

He sighed. 'Let's go to bed', he said as cheerfully as he could.

As he took hold of her visible wrist, to turn her back into the room ahead of him, she freed herself. He had halted automatically to let her turn. Instead she took a pace forward which brought her up against him in a style which would have reminded even an aspirant art student that there was a bit more to a woman than a one-dimensional shape. The little sister of the hills might not have found peace and the fulfilment of her desires but she had the outward equipment necessary to assist her. He rather gathered that she wished to find out about something connected with Ferdy's instruction.

Although he waited to let her think more rationally about it she gave no sign of being peculiarly fascinated by rationality. There were occasions when the male chauvinist beast aware of a desirable young woman stirring against him, slowly, provocatively, conscious of how her warm breath quickened as a result of his nearness to her while she indulged her hands more freely than a Victorian governess with inhibitions, really thought she deserved the fate she either sought or risked. Instead he tilted her head back and kissed her mouth. This she enjoyed. Her response, if indeed it was she who responded rather than himself, suggested this house too must ignite. He had seldom encountered a woman more determined to ensure she enjoyed herself. None could have done more to drive self-discipline from the susceptible male mind and jam it with other constrains or to have torn up her female insurance policy and tossed the fragments over an unseen but obvious windmill.

She gave far better than she got. His polite caution merely increased her resolute attack.

Abruptly her mood changed. The Amazon fled, the weak toy of man's desires unable to resist his assault on her frailty took over. She clung to him like a sailor clinging to a bit of wreckage after being in the drink for ten days. Only her clinging hands had strength while her legs seemed to crumple and her mouth hung onto his as if he had nailed it there. Women, he thought yet again, were very tricky customers. No ordinary boy like himself had a chance.

At length she gained some strength in her legs and drew back her head though her body still communicated a restlessness far better than you could risk during a tango at the Starlight Roof or the local Palais de Dance. For at least five seconds whole she could have raised the roof with an almighty scream. None came. She waited.

Into each agent's life a little calculated risk must come. He needed someone on his side if only for possible events. At present he would have willingly accepted the companionship of that appalling bore, Dr Watson of Baker Street, an individual almost entirely devoid of intelligence. Instead he had to rely on his own wits. They told him to respond to her initiative in kind.

They got along quite well. He did not advance beyond the point they had already reached but he did add variations. They seemed to gain her acceptance though she was now toying with an idea of being shy about something: that was how he divined her mood. But she did not indicate annoyance at a continuation of these enjoyable exchanges and responded willingly without any attempt to break free and scream.

When he came up for air they were both a bit breathless and more conscious of each other. Once again she took the initiative, in a form which surprised him. Holding his hand tightly, she heeled round into the house and grabbed up the lamp. At something near a gallop he was hauled into the bedroom.

She continued to take the initiative. As quickly as possible, without any sign of seeking permission, she unfastened the buttons of his shirt and turned him to where the dim light from the lamp gave her a good sight of his remarkable if scarred masculine beauty. She enjoyed his hard chest and flat stomach like a connoisseur admiring some great work of art carved in precious stone, gazing at him fore and aft agog with excitement as a young woman should be, smoothing his torso with gentle and inquisitive hands as if examining a curio. He had never known a woman so candidly fascinated by the way he was. Her fingertips searched around, absorbed by ancient scars on his chest and shoulders and went up his back to explore the scars there; he felt rather like the moon of enchantment being explored by astronauts excited by the various craters. There was no denying it. He thrilled her as if he was the highest prize at a bingo session.

At length she raised her head and stepped back a pace. He kept a hand ready to stifle a scream and the other arm coiled round her supple waist, ready to do something at the first sign of a signal to the guards muttering below. It was needless. He had never seen a woman whose face revealed such excitement quite so candidly at the mere glimpse of a male body from neck to waist. It gave him an almost humble feeling. The local boys were crazy to leave for Karachi to get their fun. The singular nature of this encounter increased as she lifted his hands and kissed them, then kissed his chest and neck, his hands again. It was fine heady stuff.

It seemed wisest to let her show how they could enjoy themselves.

The decision proved right. She charted the course faultlessly, and knew exactly what she should do while he was in no position to wait until the nearest vicar could hasten up to give advice. The resolute intensity she put into each phase implied a conviction that they were united by some long foretold destiny.

As he settled for compliance rather than risk the hellish fury he found himself beginning to take the situation seriously. It was off-key, something out of line with what he accepted as reality but this could well be an aspect of basic reality for her here among the people of this village. Now that he was in Turikrun he had to do what the Turkrunis did. His need was to remain high in her favour until he found a means of leaving the valley. And co-operated with a willingness which ensured their comprehension of each other was more memorable than a chore.

They came to a moment when he raised her head briefly to ease the long hair up from her neck and push it off her forehead. Her eyes were closed, her face smoothed in a stillness which seemed to be poised, as he looked down at her. 'You won't understand this but try to remember the word-sound,' he whispered as he stroked her 'A great woman writer once told her daughter "You are near the age when women do many stupid things; I beg you, do them with great enthusiasm".'

He could have saved his breath. She did. With her mouth tight against his shoulder and her hands talking more candidly than well-tongued words.

When he awoke the sun had already risen. He sat up yawning and rediscovering his face while memories of the night filtered into his mind. Eyes still shut, he moved his head cautiously from side to side. He discovered nothing which boded ill or bore him malice. His headache had vanished. Inside his skull was the familiar bag of cottonwool. Nothing worse; the night's events had not noticeably damaged him. If anything his nerves were calmer. The holes were still there in his memory, great damnable pits down which parts of himself had vanished, but they held less alarm for him than at any previous hour.

He yawned again and shoved up his eyelids. Almost immediately he discovered that he had been wrong about this companion. Quite wrong. But how could he have known how wrong without a guide to warn him!

9

They were evidently still alone though that gave him no discernible grounds for consolation. He heard male and female voices full of early morning bustle passing by below but none near or stationary. As he stretched his arms he sniffed at air coming into the house through the other room and detected a hint of the sweetish smoke of goats'–dung fires. If other Turikrun houses were like this one, and he imagined all of them had a similar construction, their domestic heating came from a fire in the centre of the main room beneath a small vent in the ceiling. No other smell attracted his attention. There were no other sounds. His head did not protest at having to wake up. After recent mornings that might have been something to cheer about.

'Hi,' he said and rubbed a hand over his sleep-slack face.

This sparkling lead produced no bright response.

His companion knelt on a corner of the foot of the ancient camp-bed watching him steadily. The house was pleasantly warm so she had not bothered to dress and faced him from an angle where the vague light reminded his male senses that she was a woman of fine substances able to stimulate basic instincts without reliance on words. Her gaze never wavered. No hint of a smile or reminiscent glint brightened her face. She would have been an admirable model for one of those attractive shapes chipped out by Rodin except that her thin left hand wobbled alarmingly under the weight of an old Colt

.45 revolver pointed at his navel or chest or face as if undecided which might be the best target.

He did his best to fly into a great calm and smiled cheerfully. 'You'd better give me that thing,' he said and held out his hand.

It did not escape his attention that she shook her head before he reached towards the weapon.

After a long moment in which he tried to wake up his mind while they studied each other intently he tried another approach. 'Is it a fine morning outside?' he asked and pronounced each word carefully.

The woman nodded casually.

He always liked to be sure about things. 'I slept jolly well, like a log, all night,' he said at a more rapid pace. 'I hope you slept well too.'

She nodded and for an instant the reminiscent glint was there as she partly lidded her eyes and her lips held a brief smile which hinted at her satisfaction about something. Well, there was his answer, he told himself. It made her a far more dangerous individual than he had imagined; any woman here, any authentic valley woman, who understood English could not be dismissed as just an attractive woman with a healthy appetite for experience. The revolver continued to wave like a fan but never strayed far enough to encourage him. He knew she had the strength to pull the trigger if she felt in the mood. It surprised him that she held the gun in her left hand. He had no recollection of her being lefthanded.

It required an effort but somehow he managed to yawn despite odd sensations in each region threatened by, one, the revolver, and, two, her physical ability to control any nervous twitch in the finger coiled round the trigger. Most unwisely, she had taken off the safety catch while he slept.

Obviously the woman felt tense too. When he rubbed his ribs as if they detected a chill in the air rather than a sort of paralysis born of fear, she shuddered in a most alarming fashion. He watched it go all the way down from her shoulders and chest to her forearms and hands. A weakness came into the gaze which never left him.

He tried another line of argument. 'There are certain forms of female spider which eat their mates directly they have been together and ensured that the female reproduces,' he said. 'Isn't nature odd? Not only about such items as that. I enjoyed being with you. You are a very desirable woman. As a woman you would make any man happy and content. Are you going to act like one of those spiders?'

Although he spoke rapidly and changed the inflexion of his voice from the casual to the intent and on to a form of direct-ness, she comprehended each sentence as she heard it. At the end she shook her head quickly. The expression in her eyes changed and seemed to be a plea for understanding.

He needed some of that himself.

'Put the gun on the bed and let's talk,' he said.

She shook her head again and raised her right hand and flapped it down a couple of times as if to tell him to speak more quietly.

Silk detected worry in her eyes as she fumbled about the bed on her right side and picked up three ties which lay beside her thigh. He had been too busy watching her and the gun since he awoke to pay attention to anything else. She tossed the ties towards him as if giving him a present of something she had bought in an irrational moment. If so, she had got them off a stall in a *suq* for he saw signs of them having been used. Many men would have welcomed them with delight, but the bold colourful non-designs of broken eggs mingled with grass and blood, the world's last tumultuous sunset in its scarlet and orange and white hot fury, and a purple and mauve fairground sign under a revolutionary sky, would have suited television news-readers more than himself. Even in these circumstances he disliked them.

He smiled his best. 'Very nice indeed,' he said admiringly as he inspected them. 'Silk too, by Jove. Very expensive. What's the VAT on silk here? I—'

The revolver had jerked up menacingly though she could have no knowledge of value added tax. Then deep inside the morning fog which clouded his mind an unseen penny dropped into place. He looked at her. 'Silk'? he said quietly.

They watched each other like professional wrestlers circling for an advantageous position. Her eyes asked a question which would make him certifiable if he answered without some form of preliminary safeguard. It proved quite a tussle but eventually she weakened. Perhaps the good sense she had shown until now told her that he had most to lose by open committal.

Unsurely her right hand fumbled behind her hips. When it came into sight again it had closed over something which was small enough for her hand to be almost completely shut. The question in her eyes became more obvious and she clearly did not intend to show him what her hand contained until he provided some form of answer. He had no idea of how to respond short of risking failure to keep some appointments with life which he hoped to attend whole and in good condition.

After some inner qualms he nodded. At once the woman's hand unfolded. On the palm lay a tiny bell. It had no unusual features. It was just a little bell of some inferior yellowish-grey alloy with two imperfect circular indentations as ornaments near the base of its slightly flared trumpet; it had a screw-on handle of cheap soft wood shaped rather like the bishop's mitre in an ordinary chess set and with a little hole in the top. He had seen tons of similar bells in *suqs* and bazaars all over Asia and along the North African coast. Women tied them around the necks of domestic animals and children likely to stray, in order to have an idea in which direction their wearer had gone. Some hopeful individuals attached one or more behind whatever door or flap protected their rest to give a kind of alarm if it were opened unexpectedly. On her shapely hand it resembled a cheap trinket. A bell and three silk ties.

He raised his eyes and nodded noncommitally to hide a sudden surge of excitement. Anything might happen. He hoped this would produce information of what situation his vacant brain had stumbled into. The other possibility held no attraction for him.

They went silent listening to an explosion of male voices at the bottom of the steps outside. Swiftly the woman reached forward to scoop up the ties and somehow wrap them around the bell and then she scrambled off the bed, still covering him with the old Colt, and stuffed them out of sight beneath the main bedclothes. The men continued to talk without any sound of footsteps climbing up to the house. While they waited the woman took their own private problem two steps closer to some form or other of solution. First she walked three paces forward and bent to put the gun out of sight under the pillows. Then, without straightening, she held up both hands and closed a thumb over the little finger of her right hand and folded them, leaving seven fingers and the other thumb erect for some seconds. He nodded and waited. Gently, though with familiarity, she used a forefinger to touch places of wrinkled skin on his chest and shoulders, then lifted his left arm to touch two others on his back. Eight places in all; all scars. That explained why her hands had explored his body with fierce insistence during the night, fingertips searching for evidence of identity which only nakedness could provide. Bell knew the location of eight scars he had acquired; on the last mission they undertook together they had paused to bathe in the first river they found, both of them filthier than camels, and later recalled how they picked up this scar as a memento of that place, and this one from somewhere else. Only Bell here could have told her where to search because here only Bell knew. Her uncertainty could be due to other, more recent scars.

A change in the voices outside brought him back to the immediate situation. He shifted aside to make room for her and coiled an arm round her waist, pulling her down alongside him.

This time they co-operated without misgiving. She was a very sinuous woman, coiling alongside him as if she were a *haura* sent down from the Muslim *janni*, Paradise, to loll on this sumptuous silk-covered *diwan* in a shaikh's *ha'reem* and devote herself to his little whims. Several minutes passed while they waited. He made excellent use of them. A momentary flicker of her eyes turning aside under heavy lids as she heard the praise of his various tributes probably came as close as she would ever come to a blush. Then they heard two of the guards tramp off, voices trailing behind them as they shouted some witticisms in Polish. As she drew a calmer breath he took the occasion to kiss her mouth. He saw no reason not to enjoy himself and seek to continue on a friendly basis.

He succeeded. When Wakhia moved away her breathing was noticeably more unsteady than it had been since he awoke. She let him see a feminine grimace of regret at the abandonment of what she too thought a good idea. She got off the bed and went over to where her gown hung on a bent wire hanger outside an ancient wardrobe. He watched her open the long skirt of the gown by folding it back until it revealed an envelope pinned inside. She took out the pins and let the skirt fall back into position before she came back to him, and held out the envelope. The front had the initials D.S. He tore it open. The letter inside consisted of two sheets of the sort of delicate birds'-egg blue notepaper you expected to get from a maiden aunt when you were a schoolboy and he recognised the sprawly handwriting at once.

It had been written hastily but kept to the point:

Dear D:

I haven't much time to put you in the picture of what has been going on here but will try. Nearly ten months ago a band of eight or nine West-type hippies came here to start a colony. More followed them. They were welcomed enthusiastically by local women, increasingly manless and desperate to do something about it before the wells dry up; it's mainly to do with fear they'll lose racial identity or die off childless. I'll explain later. The hippies seemed natural after what you can see in Katmandu and Kabal. There are now between seventy and eighty. But less than twenty are genuine hippies, junkies on the hard, mostly from New York, London, Amsterdam. The others are Coms of Polish, East German, Italian, Spanish descent, with two Syrians. They have one of the fake religions everybody accepts at face value nowadays as natural and fashionable for those who opt out of societies without faith and gone sour for the younger people. It's a cute line for the Kremlin to exploit. They're storing bomb material, rifles, ammunition, detonators, etc., in an empty house down the valley alongside one they've rigged up as a radio station. The stuff comes from somewhere in Afghanistan or from the Russian side of the Oxus. They plan to overthrow the govt. here. You know what that'd do. They've been jamming my calls back to L. but from the hills I managed to hear you were on the way here.

I told our little friend in Rawalpindi. I asked him to tell L. without delay. He never told him the full story. One Com got drunk here one night, mistook me for one of their brothers, and boasted how our little friend had "run double" for years. His woman is a Russ from the Caucasus, not what we were led to believe at all. Her family was one of those shoved in when Stalin deported the local people to Central Asia. Our little friend takes his orders from the leader here, Ferdy, a Hungarian, and has been told to lead you or anyone coming here into a trap. They think you'll arrive as yourself because L. never told them who would come. The drunk Com told me. Our friend will tell L. you had an accident on your way here. As far as I could gather, nobody expects you to get here. Knowing you, I do.

I have to get out now in case I'm wrong and you don't arrive. They'll try to get me before you get here. Ferdy shot the drunk Com, Hrynkiewicz, who talked to me. It'll take me two-three days to get things arranged here ready for the journey – I'll add other details to this letter before I run for it, to let you know what I've done. If I fail to get out attend to the Rawalpindi friend and his women. They've done us a lot of harm – this is something else I'll have to tell you later because I only learned about it from the drunk Com.

I'm leaving this with a woman you can trust. She'll know how to recognize you. Nobody here pays her much attention because a woman who has a physical defect – she's dumb – is not a marketable property and her parents died when she was a kid. An old aunt brought her up. She's highly intelligent and I taught her English. Bring her out with you and give me a few hours in case I can get back, then run for it.

Luck,   G.B.

Silk read the letter twice while he listened for any outside sound likely to herald a visitor. He was conscious of the girl moving about the room as she dressed and prepared for the day. At no point did she attempt to interrupt him, attending to her own concerns while he thought over what Bell told him. The effort to think on so early, rather like diving in at the deep end without having had a swimming lesson, tugged at his nerves, bothered his mind, but did not restart his headache. At present that seemed like an achievement of sorts.

The first paragraph made sense. He understood about the hippies. They had a problem; how could they feel genuine individuals in a world which reduced them to ciphers at an ever-increasing pace? He also understood the problem faced by the women; whatever the acquired tastes of some women in centres of Babel-civilization elsewhere, in such communities as these a woman would never solve her short-time and long-time problems outside of being a female entity. Those points were easy to understand. So was the woman's intention in lying in wait for him to arrive and her own enforced method of identifying him, though it encouraged him that they had advanced splendidly from that mundane commencement.

The bother in his mind started on other points. Who was 'our little friend' in Rawalpindi? How long had the 'little friend' run double, meaning been a double agent? What information had he passed over to the Russians? Who was the Russ woman? Why had Bell assumed that he would recognize them without their being named? He assumed that Bell had not named them in order to ensure that the woman wandering about the room around him did not know and therefore could not talk in order to save herself if it came to that. But he had no recollection at all of a 'little friend' in Rawalpindi or of his Russ woman.

He sat still racking his brains in attempts to remember. None succeeded. They had disappeared down one of the holes in his mind. To the best of his knowledge at this precise moment he had never known a man and woman who lived in Rawalpindi and who were friends, meaning accepted as reliable associates, of Bell and himself. But they obviously existed. And while they did he was in danger. So was Bell, if he was still alive.

His mind went on to the plot developing here. This was easier. He understood its broad outline. Bell was correct; he knew what its success would mean. It had been going on for a long time. It had some similarity to the problems caused by the Qurds in Northern Iraq and Iran. Here in these hills and all down the western side of Pakistan were revolutionaries who had long claimed they were not Pakistanis or Afghans though they preferred the Afghans. Years ago they had tried to set up a separate state to be called Pakhtunistan; it had been backed by Afghan military leaders. The plot failed and the ringleaders went underground. The failure of the West Pakistan leaders to gain victory in East Pakistan and its subsequent emergence as the independent state of Bangladesh restarted the separatist movement.

It had reappeared with new vigour. Its leaders, men now grey-headed and urged on by younger and more reckless colleagues, emerged from hideouts in Kabul and Moscow and the Libyan capital of Tripoli to resume their plot to create a revolution. They had introduced changes.

They proposed to call their separate state Pushtunistan. The old name of Pakhtunistan carried the smell of failure to too many local nostrils. They intended to split the long narrow country of Pakistan virtually down the middle and give the western half the new name. Their campaign opened with gunfights in the area, the assassination of moderate local leaders and officials loyal to the government in Islamabad, followed by armed raids on loyalist villages. This followed the favourite Asian pattern of gaining support through intimidation.

All was not well among them.

Their leaders were divided. Whatever they were called, nationalists or terrorists, conspirators or crusaders, they intrigued endlessly against each other. In the main a three-way power struggle split their surface unity. One section, that represented here in Turikrun, was Russian-led and Russian-supplied. It followed the old Kremlin formula of building solidly for something which might not be achieved for a hundred years but the power-base was intended to last longer. Another section, oldfashioned, traditional in its limited aims, was led by men whose sole intention was to see the area incorporated into Afghanistan whether the rulers there wanted it or not. The third and most violent section was led by Tripoli-oriented Muslims, associates of the Libyan leader Colonel Gaddafi who held that modern Westerners should pay for what their ancestors did or were assumed to have done in previous centuries to earlier Muslims. Each group had it spies in the other two. In local manoeuvres for power each group had murdered prominent members of the other groups.

Silk had long thought the whole thing very typical of Old Muslim politics. Only the weapons and methods had changed. The psychology was identical with historical precedent. So were the methods used by the Russians, following the methods employed by Czarist agents who played 'the Great Game' in this area against the British over a hundred years ago in their hope to enlarge the Russian Empire by turning local people against the British.

Just at present the West as a whole hoped that some miracle would cause the revolutionary leaders to vanish.

The West was in a mood to hope for miracles. None of its politicians of any hue, its endlessly threatening trade union speech-makers who claimed every threat was a plea for justice for weak and oppressed men, not even the gay priests of various denominations, or the television and radio pundits, were able to solve the West's problems of finance or prices or world food shortages or the mounting energy crisis; for their part, the Russians never mentioned such things, preferring to pretend that they were unaffected by such non-Com ailments.

Consequently the West chose to ignore events in Pakistan. Hence Bell had worked alone and in great danger. That was wrong. In the opinion of Silk and others, it was short-sighted.

A sixteen-year-old schoolboy could see the dangers which the politicians and their sparring partners chose to ignore.

One: the problem would not go away. Two: the revolutionaries would not let the differences undermine their resolve. They would become more ruthlessly determined not to let others snatch victory from them. They would wait until they achieved their objective. Three: they would then seek means to eliminate their rivals by the usual methods of assassination.

Finally, the establishment of a Pushtunistan state would create a whole series of dangers for people far removed from the actual area.

Almost without realizing it, he got off the bed as he thought and started to dress while his mind grappled with dangers which could easily result from a shift of power here. For reasons known only to herself, Wakhia came over and waited until he became aware of her and then kissed him. Momentarily he forgot other things because it was a strange salutation. Its touch of passion was overlaid by what felt like a sort of fierce regret which was positively incestuous. It was as if they were brother and sister and she wished they were strangers. She fitted herself to him so that they had maximum physical awareness of each other, a deliberate goad though she kept it under control. Then she gave him a sad little smile. She went away, leaving him to contemplate what a hostile Pushtunistan could easily mean to others.

To begin with, India would be virtually cut off from the West. So would her eastern neighbours from which Western influence had already gone, without noticeable improvement. And India had steadily increasing problems, economic and financial, aggravated by the joy her sons took in multiplying the population. Isolation could precipitate a Maoist-style revolution.

The situation on the other side of Pushtunistan would be

worse for adjacent countries and for the West. Since the bloody military coup in Afghanistan a short while ago, undoubtedly engineered and executed by the hundreds of Russian military advisers in the Afghan army and the Russian ambassador in Kabul, Afghanistan was a naked Asian Czechoslovakia which could fall under Russian military rule on any pretext to repel imperialists of non-Russian origin. Iran would be considerably weakened. She had Russia on her north. East and west were countries which did not share her type of the Muslim faith; doctrinal issues could be worked up to a pitch which reduced Ulster violence to the dimension of a Madhatter's Tea-Party. The reason was twofold. Iran had oil and the West had an energy problem. The West needed to run industry and basic communications, have heat and light, and Russia intended to bring down Britain through a combination of fuel shortage and industrial strife and the takeover of the Labour Party.

Silk and his friends had often discussed the possibility of such a situation. They had to. The Middle East, particularly the Persian Gulf area from Iran and Kuwait down to the Indian Ocean, meant oil. And while Western politicians danced happily through their careers and insignificant speeches of how to solve the problems they had created, Russia had gone steadily ahead with her plan to take control of the Middle East and its oil.

The good guy figure of Brezhnev who tried to disarm American politicians in Washington with a little theatrical 'business' with a glass of champagne and the holier-than-thou Gromyko who flew into Helsinki on angel wings to plead that everyone else should unite in eternal peace and love and blind faith in the word of the Kremlin would not deceive a mentally retarded child.

Nothing had or would lessen Russian determination to get control of the Middle East. They constructed power-bases anywhere – Egypt, Syria, Kabul, Aden, Yemen, among the

Palestinians – to exploit each exploitable hostility in order to dominate what remained of the world's oil under the dust and frenzy of the Muslim world. So if Pushtunistan was created there would not be a single safe head anywhere from Tripoli to Delhi as thousands of ambitious Muslim politicians sprang onto the Kremlin bandwagon and got ready to slaughter those now in power in the region. And their dearest friend, the biggest arms-manufacturer and armament-salesman in history, was Com Russia.

It could happen easily. Why not? The troubled people of Turikrun provided an ideal community for a group of male revolutionaries to take over, the peculiar problems of the women made them particularly vulnerable, and the isolated valley was an ideal setting for a base.

There were other reasons he could see for Russia to try to take positive action in this region now. The West had a maximum of ten years before its energy crisis reached the point of no return if it had not found alternative sources. A takeover of Pakistan would be much nearer if a Kremlin–ruled Pushtunistan could be established. And the pressure was on Russia too. The Kremlin was poised on a see-saw. She had either to dominate Europe in order to turn around and face China or go on spending vast sums of money on an army and air force to knock over China before she took on Europe. Hence her attempts everywhere to weaken European initiative and gain control of Europe's present life-blood, Middle East oil.

That was the vast impersonal scene with its involved issues which would be worked out for good or ill by people. Here, by the people of Turikrun and their visitors. Including Bell, if he was still alive. The woman moving silently around him about her early morning chores. And himself.

He saw complications among the last three too which he would sooner not have had to contemplate.

He accepted in good faith that Wakhia was dumb. He had no proof of it. A woman could discipline herself to fill almost any role for a limited time if she had to do so when reasons made other things unimportant to her. She would lie or murder or sleep with anyone, and cheat and betray.

His confused and holed mind needed proof about her and he very much doubted that he would get it until it was too late. He also needed proof that Bell had written the letter voluntarily. It had been some time since Bell and he last met. Men change. Many men wrote or said things to escape prolonged torture; look at the prisoners of war in North Korea and American POWs in North Vietnam, to think of only the two latest examples. Nonetheless, the letter rang true and it fitted in with the incident he had witnessed on the hill opposite, unless that was an elaborate piece of hocus-pocus. But why should anyone here stage such a scene for him, particularly if they did not know who he was? And then there was the crashed chopper on the hillside here.

His mind became confused as he faced the problems which enmeshed him, but he forced himself to go on looking at them. Who the hell was 'our little friend from Rawalpindi'? He knew Rawalpindi. Who didn't? As towns went around here, he liked it. He had no recollection of having friends there, male or female.

Swann?

Swann.

His mind cleared as he thought about Swann. He would never forget Swann, an older man than himself, the man who gave him the invaluable groundwork an agent needed to operate anywhere among Arabs and across Asia. Nor would he forget how he found Swann in a Cairo alley, dying from being beaten up and kicked to bloody pulp by Egyptian Coms. He would never forgive himself for letting it happen; he should have found a system of contact to prevent it. At odd moments, mostly when he joined the four a.m. brigade lying awake with their miseries, it came back to claw and tear at him ... the murmurs which come from the past ... one door shuts, another opens. That was when he first met Fathiya. Murmur.

He frowned. Why he felt the name should have significance for him? Murmur. No, it meant nothing.

'Our little friend from Rawalpindi.'

He rubbed a hand down his face. If Bell was telling the truth, he should know both the friend and his Russ Com woman from the Caucasus. But in Rawalpindi.

For an instant it seemed as if he was on the verge of some significant recollection. It put a feeling of sickness into his stomach, but he forced himself to ignore that. He had a sensation of looking at brightly coloured bits and pieces which seem to form together in a pattern inside one of those reflecting mirror gadgets kids looked at before television socked the world into a nightly stupor. A male voice beside him in daylight. His legs walking. A chopper circling overhead. Men muttering.

The bits faded and dissolved and he was looking down the black holes again.

Exasperated, miserable, he undid his shirt cuffs and turned them back, turned them over again and rebuttoned them. He knew several of the things he wanted to do even though most of them might be unprofitable. What he most wanted to do was to sit out on the balcony in the brightness and get back his memory. That could not be. He had to be busy to avoid suspicion among the guards and to prevent the woman from thinking he was weak about something. Those were risks he had to steer clear of at present.

He paused in his wander round the room and tried to get the tasks ahead of him into a sequence of importance. As he did so he caught sight of the woman standing motionless beside the bed, watching him as if trying to read his thoughts. A faint smile momentarily relaxed her lips. Already they had drifted back into being strangers. He smiled at her like a man smiling at a woman who has given him reason to face another dawn with pleasure and who still had intimate memories of her sharp in his mind. If an agent felt frustrated when he had company it was always wisest to smile. Still smiling, he went across to her but changed his intention and sat down, pulling her down so that she half-lay across his legs with her back against his arm. This too frustrated him. He would love to question her, drive her replies into a corner so that either nuances in her voice or an unguarded expression might tell him how to frame later questions which would prove her to be a liar. Everything in this situation seemed to be weighted against him.

And nothing in her stilled face as she looked up at him provided any help. He noted that her skin was very fair for anyone of this region. Her eyes were blue. The colour of her thick hair was a dark chestnut. He gazed at her with the fascinated absorption of a besotted lover, unable to think of any more positive tactic open to him. His deliberate, bruising occupation of her lips merely provided that he had been right in two utterly useless opinions about her. She was devastatingly healthy. Someone had told her that a woman should respond to this aspect of the male chauvinist beast with gusto and turn it into an event.

That was all.

She sat up directly he released her. For an instant she let him note that her admirable nostrils were flared. Then she took his hand and made him get up to accompany her into the other room.

Yes, by golly, he was frustrated.

Breakfast did not take long. They had eggs and slices of the unleavened bread somewhere between *ch'patti* and *nan*. As at their meal last evening she tasted everything before he did. Belatedly it dawned on him that this might have a more practical, and less folk-romantic, purpose than he had attached to it originally. Her deliberate actions and her subsequent glance at him could mean that she tasted each item in search of poison. Or to let him believe she searched for poison.

He nodded acknowledgement without being unduly impressed. Efforts to reassure him always had the reverse effect. He distrusted them.

Directly the meal ended he led the woman back into the other room and made her sit on the bed while he examined the revolver. It was a heavy old wartime weapon, too awkward to lug around except in a hip holster. There was evidence that it had gone through a period of prolonged neglect, the proof clear around the barrel and finger-guard, but someone had lately brought it into good working condition. He assumed Bell must have bought it in Chitral, to have a second weapon available at some concealed place or in case his modern automatic was stolen; men like Bell did not lose their guns. He tipped the bullets into one hand and touched them with the other forefinger as he looked at the woman.

'More?' he said quietly.

She nodded and went across the room to an old chest similar to one he had seen in a Mongol yurt in Central Asia. While he watched she manipulated a sort of false stave inside the curved lid and he saw it slide to one side; from a narrow cavity she produced a narrow metal-bound box. She closed the opening and shut the lid and brought the box to him. When he opened it he found nineteen bullets inside. Nineteen in addition to the six which the revolver already contained did not represent much defence against the local opposition but it was better than nothing. He always believed in looking on the dark side. It saved one from nasty little shocks.

He reloaded the revolver and closed it and snapped on the safety-catch and put the other bullets back into the cardboard box and sat looking at the chest. No, he didn't like the arrangement. It was an obvious place for anyone to search for a weapon. Moreover, in an emergency the box would be awkward to get at quickly. He looked around the room for a suitable hiding place. None of the few that he saw were suitable.

Abruptly he went still, thinking he heard a conversation between voices at the foot of the steps. The woman also heard it and appeared to interpret it as he did, her hand reaching for the cardboard box. Neither of them moved.

Several minutes passed before the voices ceased. He did not budge, listening intently. It crossed his mind unpleasantly that if they were caught unawares in a moment such as this either the woman could be revealed as part of a hoax to trap them or, if genuine, her nerve might crack. One style and another he disliked the situation he was in more and more.

As the silence lengthened he looked up at Wakhia. Her face was expressionless, her eyes watchful as if expecting him to take decisions. Well, there was no alternative: he had to rely on her apparent good faith. The wide sweep of his arm embraced the whole house as he looked at her.

'Is this house yours?' he asked in a lowered voice.

She nodded. The hand which held the box of cartridges copied the action of his arm as if to give an affirmative emphasis. He touched the revolver and the box with his other hand.

'Is there a safer place where we can hide these?'

She nodded emphatically and took the revolver from him, then beckoned him to follow her. As he got up she went round the bed and crouched down in front of the plain wood planks which formed the walls: the walls suggested that the builder had watched houses being built in Chitral in the last century. At the pressure of her hand a half plank swung open on hinges unseen from the outside. Behind it one of the horizontal logs which formed the outside of the house had a hollowed space; it could have been the place where the houseowners hid their few valuable trinkets. The woman turned, a question in her eyes. He nodded. She laid the box on the base and took the weapon from him and placed it on top. He thought it far from ideal but it would have to do, certainly for the time being. The woman turned to him again and held out her hand, another question in her eyes. Momentarily he failed to comprehend what she meant. Then he realized she wanted to hide Bell's letter with the other things. He shook his head, motioning her to close the compartment. As she turned to him he took her hand and led her back in to the other room and there she stood watching as he burned the letter and envelope and ground the ash to powder under the heel of a shoe. That ensured that no one could use the letter against him if it was indeed genuine.

He stood up thinking of things which needed to be done. Something else had to be done first to wake up his mind to be able to cope with them; he made washing movements with his hands near his face and chest. Wakhia nodded and pointed towards the window, then her right hand made a scraping motion under her jaw and over her chin. He shook his head.

'I haven't got a razor', he told her.

She ran into the other room and returned within seconds with an old safety razor, a new blade, and soap, even soap. It was probable that Bell had got the new blade on his last visit to Chitral. Otherwise Silk saw no valid reason for the woman having them in her house. Bell might have told her to keep them in case he arrived here without them.

'Do we wash in one of the streams?' he asked.

She nodded.

Two armed guards followed close behind as the woman led the way through the village. The villagers were candidly curious about him, pausing to stare as if he was an accident. There was something in that. The brothers and disciples of Ferdy were equally interested though they had obviously been ordered not to display curiosity.

Once again the woman's face wore an expression of pride as if delighted that she had 'earned the right' to a man. Was he wrong or was her expression even more satisfied than when she led him into the village last evening? True, he was a rare prize for any woman but he preferred her to keep the joy of ownership to herself.

He knew himself at considerable risk in this already warm sunshine. Accidents with guns did happen to the nicest people. It could happen to him and the woman at any instant. They were clay pigeons for every fool under instruction. He wished he had decided to stay dirty and unshaven.

10

Hour after hour the morning sunshine illuminated a village where everyone behaved with astounding ordinariness. Perhaps acted would be a more apt description than behaved. It was very strange.

Silk had stayed for varying lengths of time in a good many remote villages but he had never encountered one like this. In those other villages although daily chores had to be done, there was always a group of older men or women or younger children who gathered to stare at and discuss anything new or strange. Within a short space of time Turikrun had witnessed several such items. Up on the hillside was the crashed helicopter. Silk knew it must have crashed recently or no one would have been searching its debris when he reached the village; moreover, it had the look of a recent crash. No Turikruni paid it attention; even the small boys ignored it. Last evening a man had been killed or injured on the opposite hillside in sight of everyone who paused to see the chase which ended in the event, and many had stopped to watch, yet this morning no group of old men gathered to talk and those in sight seemed to avoid each other as they wandered about in the sunshine. During the night a house had burned to the ground. He and the woman had stood together and watched scores of people hurry from their rest to watch the blaze. Yet this morning no one, not even the small boys, paid it the slightest attention. Several could have gone down to look at the still slightly smoking ruins but everyone ignored it. There could be only one logical explanation. Under their veneer of indifference the Turikruni people were frightened.

He saw no visible sign of fear as he wandered about the village in full sight of everyone and busy as a tourist with six cameras as he gazed at the pale split log houses and examined their strange ornamentation. It would have undermined his role of a trained visitor not to get around in the sunlight and fresh air, and so he had plenty of opportunity to watch for signs of fear. There were none except the indifference. But he could smell it, strong and pungent, pervasive, coming from many of the houses. The children ignored him. The women took one glance and turned away. The old men hopped out of sight as if afraid he might try to talk to them in sign language. He did not attribute this entirely to the guards who accompanied him everywhere. They were armed with Russian Kalashnikov rifles or AK47 assault rifles, depending on who accompanied him. But there had been armed guards when he arrived.

On his walks he managed to get some work done. Only the guards accompanied him; the woman had stayed behind in the house to attend to her chores. He studied the carved wood shrine-statues of ancestors, badly weathered by the climate, of heroic figures with stark faces, more centaurs than men on horses. He noted how the ends of some support beams had been carved into the heads of horses or goats by craftsmen long dead and how the top of some posts were hewn to represent blank all-seeing eyes, like those of the Buddha high up on towers or turrets of Tibetan lamaseries.

Shortly before midday he came within smell of the *mandao-jao*, the 'place of many coffins', just beyond a large irregular wood of mixed deciduous trees and flowering bushes.

The exposed coffins strewn about anyhow had large rocks on their lids. He judged this more a precaution to prevent four-footed night-predators who scavanged around from getting inside than to prevent the occupants from suddenly startling the living by a mass emergence to find out how the world had got along without them. Higher up many old coffins were open, their lids shoved aside or vanished; on the ground around them lay skulls and a litter of bones. Near the path from the village was a surprising number of new coffins. The aroma from them suggested that their inhabitants were mainly middleaged, when the body can be at its most odorous. Unless he was vastly mistaken they contained active Turikruni men, possibly some women, who had protested at Ferdy's takeover of the village. He would have liked to ask Wakhia if a number of women here had been widowed recently but if she were on the other side, as well she might be, such a question would show he was more alert than he should be and would be something for her to pass on to Ferdy. It would be foolish of him to trust her to that extent.

The two guards hovered near while he gazed at the *mandao-jao* unable to detect an extremely new coffin which might have been placed there since last evening. That provided a problem. Somehow or other in the narrowing time at his disposal he should search the new coffins to see if one contained Bell's body. He tried to memorize the position of the half-dozen whose wood looked the least affected by weather. They would provide a starting point. Yet a search might prove useless. They could have concealed Bell's body somewhere rather than attract attention to a new coffin.

A queer half-memory sagged limply through his mind as he heard the two guards whispering behind him. For an instant he seemed about to remember something. Then the sensation dissolved. He stayed still for some moments to mark the location of the two houses standing alone farther on which he took to be those referred to in the letter from Bell as the armoury and the radio station; there were no other buildings anywhere near. He would dearly like to know if Bell had managed to put time-bombs in either of them and whether the devices were faulty or set for an hour yet to come. If nothing happened in the next few hours he had to try to get into them. They were far more important than to find out if Bell's body was in the *mandao-jao*. Unless he found out that the letter had been written under pressure.

He turned on his heels and smiled wryly at the guards. 'Quite a nasty stench, isn't it?' he commented to their stony faces.

Although Ferdy had promised him such fascinating entertainments as a *shaman* walking on hot coals and the ceremony involving the boy virgins, the afternoon began as ordinarily as the morning.

After a lunch of goat's-milk cheese with bread and fresh fruit saturated with a form of local wine, the woman and he lazed on the shadowy hot balcony above a desultory mutter of guards. Later he had another walk. This time Wakhia accompanied him. Two guards trudged sullenly behind them. He indulged in a form of talking to himself, chatting enthusiastically about some form of mountain ibex which he saw leaping from crag to ledge and on to a crag high up on the distant hillside, and wondered aloud if several large birds riding the thermals high above the centre of the valley were Bonelli's eagles or some specie of hawk. It was just possible that one or other of the guards was more intelligent than he looked and might pick on such chat as proof that the uninvited guest knew something about wild creatures in such regions.

As on the morning walks Silk noted that the guards were always under scrutiny by others of Ferdy's henchmen to see if he tried to talk to them,

The landscape filled him with increasing despair. The rugged boulder-patched valley sides with their spills of talus conifer forests and sprawling deciduous woods, goat and ibex tracks higher up, human paths below, the many twisted channels worn by run-off from the mountains, were distinctly unhelpful. He failed to detect one easy route back to the one by which he came here. None offered a temporary safety plus a minimum demand on stamina. His stomach told him that they faced a tricky journey back.

As they went towards the village again the black bearded figure of Hawks bore down on them from a group of men whose appearance and bearing suggested they were members of Ferdy's élite, the disciples. Ripples in the hair around Hawk's nose suggested he was smiling at them.

'You'd better have an early meal,' he said. 'The women will dance this evening. Especially for you, Doctor.' He sounded nauseatingly coy. 'They are looking forward to it. Your little friend will have to keep an eye on you.'

'How very kind of them!' Silk said in his most gracious tone. 'Have you seen my friend yet? Mr Bell?'

Hawks shook his head. 'Not yet,' he replied cheerfully, 'but don't worry Doctor. He's probably somewhere about.'

He went across to a group of disciples as Silk and the woman went on back to her house.

As the afternoon wore on the village went silent. Silk sat on the balcony watching the scene while Wakhia prepared them a meal. He saw no women anywhere; presumably they were all indoors preparing a meal for their men or their families. There was not a single *onjesta-mosh* in sight; no doubt their mothers had called them in. A few old men hung about but still seemed to avoid each other. When Wakhia came to fetch Silk for the meal he could smell fear in the village more strongly than at any time during the day. No trace of it showed in her eyes but her face was taut.

They were among the first to reach the clearing where the dance was to be held. It had obviously been a corner of one strip of conifer forest in previous times. As they neared it Silk whispered, 'Is this the usual place for the dance and other events?' and saw Wakhia nod slightly, a mere inclination of her forehead.

She led them to one of the many fallen or felled trunks

lying in front of the clearing which served as seats and provided uninterrupted views over what was a natural stage. Their single guard ambled over to a nearby trunk and yawned boredom as he sat down, scratching a thin black fringe beard which dangled limply beneath his pale face.

Silk glanced round as the woman adjusted her skirt. On each side of the clearing were old carved ancestor funerary statues, the wood long since faded and weathered. They bore some resemblance in atmosphere to the little religious shrines chanced on in Italian country roads of the north or of old Roman avenue busts on small pedestals. Most of them were partly sheltered by trees, some by piles of boulders tossed here when the unquiet earth's birth-pangs squeeezed up the mountain ranges of Middle Asia aeons ago, and all the statues had a distinct family resemblance. The head of each was roughly carved from a single block of wood and was dominated by the same facial characteristics: a deep heavy rounded jaw, flat unshaped cheeks which fell sheer from deeply-set eye-sockets under jutting foreheads, straight noses, jug ears which jutted out like handles, thin and shapeless little lips which gave an atmosphere of fastidious primness. They were as distinctive as the Polynesian carvings on Easter Island.

Silk was fascinated. There were other similarities. Not one statue represented a woman. They were all unmistakably male, body flat and angular under tunic or jersey and knee-length kilt. Each head was topped by the same distinctive hat, half-Biblical turban, half Hittite warrior's helmet, the circular shape rising to a pointed top. The complete absence of a female figure explained the indifference Turikrun males showed to their women and the conceits of the pale little *onjesta-mosh* who were supposed to be the pride of their warrior ancestors.

'I wonder why?' he queried aloud.

Unexpectedly Oliver Hawks sat down on the log beside him. 'What was that?' he asked with a joviality which creaked.

Silk did not imagine the courtesy call resulted from good

manners. He thanked his lucky stars he had just indulged one of his hobbies; it added a keener edge to his secret weapon. As he launched into a description of the statues and compared them to others he had seen a glazed expression spread over the visible parts of Hawks's face. His faltering mmmm-mmmms indicated lack of knowledge of the subject.

'There's a lot in what you say, Doctor,' he interrupted. 'You certainly know your subject. I don't know anything about it. Until Ferdy showed me the light I was just a simple ordinary industrial shop-steward.' He leaned forward to glance past Silk at the silent woman. 'How are you getting on with the lady?'

'She is a most thoughtful hostess.'

'Is she looking after you? Properly?'

'No one could ask for more. Naturally we have some problem over communication. But she is very intelligent.'

Silk spoke distinctly in the hope that she would understand the conversation clearly. If she was indeed a good friend of Bell then he owed it to her. If she worked for the other side it did no harm. He did not intend to take unnecessary risks.

Hawks nodded. 'Good good!' he exclaimed cheerfully. 'Ferdy asked me to tell you again he's sorry if her defect is causing you any bother.' He laughed. 'I wouldn't say it was a defect for a woman to be dumb. Out here, I mean. In our type of country it's a considerable handicap, of course, but not among backward people like these, eh Doctor? Maybe you've got another view of it. Well, you just came along. It could be called the luck of the draw. She won you. I hope she's more than a good cook.'

'I expect these women have a problem,' Silk commented.

Hawks gave his single short sharp bark of a laugh again. 'They certainly had until the light led Ferdy to found our community here,' he said with every sign of a man ad-libbing wildly to establish a sort of normality which was entirely beyond him. In this sort of mood, Hawks was as phoney as plastic. He had nothing of the new drop-out religious community's intensity and nothing of the hippie's verbal fierceness. No schoolboy would believe in him.

'Every small isolated group facing extinction has problems the West does not comprehend,' Silk said. 'Hence polygamy in some Saharan tribes and Egyptian communities when it was common for women to die in childbirth. Hence polyandry among Tibetan nomads and in Ladakh where the men succumb much more easily to the elements and women need two or more husbands. Indeed, hence the sacred cow of prehistoric India. As you know, Mr Hawks.'

Hawks's beard served as a very helpful camouflage. 'Exactly!' he agreed heartily. 'We appreciate your understanding of our position too, Doctor Eden. We have our troubles here.'

Silk knew he was about to be told something. That gave him heart; up to this moment they believed his cover. Otherwise they had no need to offer him a story which would amount to an excuse.

'Have you really?' he asked in a tone of disbelief. 'How strange!'

'Well, as you say, Doctor, the people here are isolated. These little boy virgins – I expect you know about them? yes, I thought so – believe that directly their "time of grace" is over and they are accepted as men, they can claim any nubile girl they want. The two *pshés*, the soothsayers, support their claim. For the last week the *pshés* have stayed in their temple, it's called a *jestak-kan*, praying to their sacred fairies, the *shawani*, to ask the gods to get rid of us. Some of the old men can be very nasty. They've killed two of our men at night. That's why we have to have guards in the village.'

Unseen, the woman's hand brushed against Silk's and went away.

Silk said, 'How very unpleasant for you' and tch-tched commiseratingly at the thought. He supposed that one of the disciples had seen him looking at the *mandao-jao* during the morning and thought he should be given a partial reason for the number of new coffins there, in case the thought had occurred to him. 'I'm sure you will overcome such problems in time.'

'Ferdy hopes so. He believes his true teaching can begin here.'

'I'm sure it will. Thank him for me for providing us with a guard. I'm most grateful. But I won't be troubling you much longer. My friends will pick me up some time tomorrow evening or the next morning, providing their helicopter doesn't delay them. Tell me, Mr Hawks, is the wind difficult here? I see one had an accident here.'

'Yes,' Hawks said, his voice flat and grey as a city pavement. 'Some of our dear brothers were killed.'

'Oh, I'm sorry.'

'They were a great loss to us all,' Hawks said sadly. 'Yes.' He glanced round as if for a distraction to his distress. 'Ah'? he exclaimed. 'Here's Ferdy. See you later, Doctor.'

He got to his feet and hurried away.

Silk glanced at the woman. At once she turned her head to look at him. A vague smile curved her lips and her eyes had the expression of those who possess in being possessed, a nice little piece of acting for all the other villagers coming onto the clearing to see and note down. No spoken words could have done better in these circumstances. Whichever side she was on she interpreted her role in public with him faultlessly. That was scarcely surprising because not all the intelligence and subtlety and deceitfulness were exclusively owned by the so-called White race, but it helped him at present. Here she was in public, a woman with a physical defect which lowered her value among her own superstitious people and caused them to put a *tabu* on her as they probably did on everything they did not fully understand, probably attributing her fault to the gods' displeasure with her, yet she had found favour with a stranger. There might be side effects in the future which could harm her or him, providing that she was genuine, but for now she was just right. Her eyes smiled at the expression in his. Then she lidded them and turned away. The smile lingered on her lips.

Silk glanced around as if he felt like one of the community.

In the bright evening light Ferdy stood with his hand raised in salutation as he faced the assembled people in each direction. The salute did bear more similarity to the Nazi salute than to a benediction. Ferdy took his time. His whole attitude suggested that if there had been a lake handy Someone Else would have a keen competitor for the walk. Silk had a shrewd idea who would sink first. It was incredible that the man could take himself so seriously in this role. But they did. Even without political intrigue and revolution, they did. With politics all of them tried to produce a holy doctrine to outdo long-established Holy Doctrines.

While Ferdy went through the motions and then spoke kindly to old people, bending over them like a curate, some fifty women who had been sitting with their disciple escorts got up and went to form a line across the centre of the clearing.

At present Silk was more interested in the group of junkies who had followed Ferdy into sight. Until now he had not seen them. Junkies they most certainly were. The only habitual drug-takers who could conceal their plight from an informed observer were those of an otherwise high intelligence who could outwardly control or conceal the tell-tale evidence of their craving. The time when they could not mask their addiction came for them too, as it did for Skid Row drunks. But these men and women were of low intellect, probably poor education, certainly lacking any self-discipline, and showed they were hooked. They straggled into full view, unsure, nervous, belligerent, twitchy, and shabby. One of them had a continuous soft scared giggle. Several smiled aimlessly.

All of them were typical of junkies who Silk had seen from

Afghanistan to Nepal. Many were probably like the old-time remittance-men who had disgraced their family in an era when respectability and family pride meant something; no doubt their families sent money to keep them away from home. Ferdy probably used them as a front, as visionaries possessed periodically by spirits, djinns, redeemed *ifrits*, and the like. The people of Turikrun probably interpreted their ravings when they were high as signs of *ecstasis*.

Silk took the woman's hand and felt over it affectionately and was rewarded by a strong pressure in return while they watched Ferdy and Hawks go slowly down the line of women like visiting VIPs inspecting a guard of honour.

Silk wondered what the Russians would not do now to win the 'Great Game' started here well over a hundred years ago when Britain was in India and Czarist troops were reducing the great wastes of Central Asia and south-west Asia to the vassal states now ruled even more firmly by the Communist Kremlin. In that early phase the Russians had beaten a tactical retreat. The withdrawal had not lasted long. Back in the nineteen-twenties the Coms had sent two spies, Vavilov and Bukinitsh, into the Pech Valley. He had forgotten the names of Muslim Russians who followed them, who settled among the tribespeople, shared their lives, married their daughters, and bred children destined to seek revolution from within. There had been some German Nazis too, seeking friends. But from the nineteen-twenties on there were always Russians. And Russia would never give up her belief that she had a right to rule the countries of this part of Asia.

He winced as his head started to ache venomously. Occasionally during the day it had grumbled when he tried to fill up the holes in his mind. Now it seemed to blur his eyesight. He had a conviction that if he could only fill up those holes the ache would vanish and he would regain both the impetus and ability to concentrate which seemed to desert him on occasion.

To his relief the dance commenced directly Ferdy had given

his blessing to all and sundry again and seated himself with obvious chief disciples of unmistakably Middle European appearance on a large tree-trunk set apart from the others. Over on the right side of the clearing someone started to play a flute. He saw it was a young girl, her hair done in long dark braids; her dark gown made her almost invisible against the tangled brown and green of the trees behind her. Within a minute another flute answered from the other side of the clearing. Almost at once a drum began a slow quiet beat. And slowly the fifty or sixty women began to dance.

They reminded Silk vaguely of the formation dance teams which caused ecstacies among habitués of Western dance-halls. The similarity was heightened by all the women wearing cowrie-shell and long-tasselled *kupis* topped by a large pom-pom, flowing Grecian-style gowns, bright woollen cummerbunds, and showing their bare ankles and feet. The dance too had marked similarities to the geometrical patterns evolved for Western amateur dance-teams. Their weaving of intricate geometric patterns was unlike anything seen in neighbouring countries. And it was a team composed solely of women; nothing like it was permitted in adjacent Muslim countries. The drum thudded only intermittently; it sounded like a hollowed-out log covered with goat-skin. Once in a while one or other of the women broke into a wordless song which matched the flutes.

At first the whole scene was comparatively clear. The women went through their paces as their female ancestors had done for centuries. They were watched in attentive silence by a highly knowledgeable audience; women like them but heavy with child, old men and women who had seen such performances throughout their lives, the girl flautists who knew exactly when to vary the tune and its pace.

As the sky paled, shadows darkened around the scene. If Silk had gone in for melodramatic exaggerations, he would have described the atmosphere as peacefully sinister. Everything became quieter. The wordless singing ceased. The drum went silent. Suddenly the flutes grew shrill and discordant as if they were sick voices calling on the moon to rise and give them strength. Then they too went still. But the women went on dancing.

He was not the only one who found the atmosphere a bit eerie. As the gloom intensified the woman's hand found his and kept tightening convulsively. Several yards away on their right one of the most heavily pregnant women laughed nervously, her voice a shrill whinny. Immediately other women gave vent to similar relief.

Suddenly Silk went very still and quiet. A sliver of memory had come back to him. The main deities of these people were Mahandeo and Jestak: Mahandeo the mighty warrior and hunter, model for the grim statues; Jestak the busy housewife who ruled family and home, children and sickness. And in times of crisis they had ruled that sacrifices be made to prevent the machinations of the local variation of Satan . . . Ferin? Farin? Varin? . . . a creature full of malevolence. Obviously the women of the valley had many dance patterns to suit either the significance of the seasons or some religious ceremony or their own moods. He would like to know which dance they were performing now.

He watched the first glint of moonlight pick the faces of the dancing women out of the swirling shadows. Simultaneously fingers started a rapid tattoo on the drum. They beat faster and faster.

Over on the other side of the audience a man started to scream hysterically.

Silk turned his head to see what caused the interruption. He felt the woman's hand cling to his. The drummer worked himself into a frenzy. Flashlights came on. Their beams swept among onlookers though the women continued to dance as if oblivious to everthing.

Across Silk's mind floated bits of memory. He seemed to

125

recall sitting at dinner with a big man and a small woman whose voice had a sharp accent. They were telling him about the gods and goddesses of this valley. A big man with sleek dark hair? A small graceful woman with an artistic temperament? Antique weapons? Peshawar? Rawalpindi? Our little friend?

He saw the beams of light steady but his mind was busy with his thoughts, trying to remember. The torchlight had picked out three or four places quite wrongly, two behind had fastened their rays on himself and the woman and threw their shadows forward on the grass in front of them. He wished they would go out so that he could think more clearly. And he wished someone would do something about the screaming man. Most flashlights had fastened on him. He had stood up among a group of the genuine hippies. He was tall and completely bald and had a ragged beard. His thin body was naked to the waistband of stained and torn khaki twill trousers and he was barefoot. His lungs seemed to hold an inexhaustible amount of air. While he screamed his narrow arms flailed the air as if mechanically operated. Abruptly he started to run towards the dancing women.

Silk wondered why nobody did anything about it. Although such events did sometimes impel weak individuals to emotional extremes they were seldom reported to have been like this. Perhaps Ferdy and his disciples and the women expected such frenzy. No one could tell what a junkie would do.

Silk watched reluctantly, annoyed at having his attention diverted. He wished to Heaven someone would do something positive instead of behaving as if the man was part of the entertainment. He wanted to think.

The scream drooped to a bubbling wet moan. As the man reached the women something gripped by his right hand shone bright in the flashlights' glow. Silk saw it was a dagger. Other spectators saw it too and women and boy virgins started to scream. It was too late for the armed guards to fire for fear of shooting some of the serenely dancing women. The man grabbed hold of one woman and tore her away from her companions. His right arm jerked up and flashed down twice. The woman fell tiredly to the ground. Instantly the man spun round, glancing from left to right as if seeking a means of escape. Then he rushed forward towards where the steady flashlights illuminated Silk and the woman.

Belatedly Silk's mind started to work. Everything about the oncoming figure told of a man gone *amok*. His soughing breath rose to another scream. Silk shook off the woman's wet hand and jerked to his feet. Abruptly the man stopped. His body crouched, tense and poised. He came on again, snarling, dribbling, the dagger carving the air. Nobody did anything; the fallen woman lay unattended, the other women continued to dance, the spectators did not want to get involved. The man continued to come on, slowly, step by step. That broke the nerve of some nearby onlookers. They clambered off the tree-trunks and took to their heels, screaming their terror. Incredibly the tireless women on the clearing went on with their geometry as if decorating a maypole tree.

Silk braced himself. He had only seen one man go *amok* before. It was not a pretty sight. On impulse he tried to take the initiative and walked forward towards the crouched and menacing junkie.

'Drop that knife!' he raved at the man. 'You hear me? Drop it! You understand?'

His action or his voice took the man as much by surprise as they took him. Together they matched the drive and ferocity shown by the man. He saw the crouching figure halt and the arms fall to its side as though the demented wretch had lost impetus and could not think. In the glow of the still steady flashlights behind the bearded face had a trancelike vacancy, the eyes glassy, saliva dribbling obscenely down from the hanging under-lip. The man seemed robbed of assurance.

Silk continued to act while he still had the slight advantage

127

of having taken an initiative through surprise. He took off as if he was on the high board and dived for the man's feet. The instinct of sheer cowardice told him that he had no alternative. He hoped that he might somehow avoid the dagger when the man regained his wits sufficiently to renew his murderous onslaught.

One of his outstretched, groping hands found one of the man's thin ankles. More by luck than judgement, his other hand bumped against the other ankle, recognized it for what it was, and clung to it. As he landed the ground knocked the air out of his body and great silvery balloons exploded in front of his eyes. Somewhere beyond a droning in his ears he heard voices screaming shrilly, women, boys, faltering old men, a gutteral shout from farther off. There were two sharp detonations. Instinct aided him again. Somehow he managed to drag the man's ankles forward while he writhed back towards the log, wrenched again and again with the strength of desperation. At the third haul the solid resistance he encountered at first had gone. The man's feet turned slowly up towards his face, soles in front. Without another sound the man thudded full-length onto his back.

Instantly he let go and scrambled breathlessly to his knees. To his half-dazed senses it seemed the logical thing to do. It proved wrong. Something which felt like a shoe kicked him at the back of the neck. He sprawled down full-length again banging his forehead on the ground. For a moment he was vaguely aware of noise and then it started to slide away from him.

11

'Are you sure you feel all right?' Ferdy asked. 'It was a very unpleasant experience. You showed great presence of mind.'

His talents were wasted up in these bleak hills. He spoke in the grave tone of a fashionable big-city *guru*, full of solicitude. The faint accent and slightly stilted English, the careful search for an appropriate word which caused tiny breaks in each sentence, lent his voice a sort of exotic flavour which was increased by the combination of darkness and moonwash sprinkled along the valley and over the clusters of houses among which they stood. With a front as a *sadhu* consoling rich white widows and impressible spinsters he could make a rich living while still serving his masters, an export version of Rasputin. The role would suit him.

'I'm fine,' Silk replied brightly. 'Just a slight headache. A short walk in this wonderful air will take care of it. If you can spare one of your friends to accompany us. I imagine Miss mmmm mmmm Wakhia is still rather upset. Nasty experience for a girl, y' know.'

'You shall have two guards.'

'Most generous of you.'

'It is the least I can do.'

'These things happen.'

'I shall not let it happen again. This must be a valley of peace.'

'Such a tragedy will prove the importance of your faith,' Silk assured him.

He could not see the faces of either Ferdy or Hawks, or of the two men with them. Since the dance ended in hysterical confusion Ferdy and his disciples had contrived to keep their faces in shadow; when they halted here they had turned so that the moonlight was behind them. He had a good idea why they chose to be eclipsed. Those who have recently learned that Robbie Burns was right about the best-laid scheme of mice and men going aft a-gley, in this case their own, tended to look petulant. Hawks had taken the additional precaution of silence.

'You are most generous to extend to us the warmth of your understanding,' Ferdy said gravely.

Silk thought it must be a dreadful strain to be always 'in character' as this guy was whenever he was in public. Several members of the Russian KGB whom he had known never came out of it, maintaining their role with even greater care in front of colleagues who would willingly rush off to report any small lapse which they imagined likely to damage a 'front' or a mission. One thing had become starkly clear. The overall warning given in Bell's letter now had the support of factual evidence.

'We will come to see how you are tomorrow morning,' Ferdy was saying. 'If you need anything in the night, call on one of your guards. Do you require any medicine for your headache, Doctor Eden?'

'I never use any medicine if I can help it,' Silk answered. He had some distaste for the idea of being given poison accidentally. 'This air will do the trick. You mustn't worry.'

Ferdy went through the same hocus-pocus form of giving a blessing which concluded their encounter last evening. When it ended he and his disciples turned slowly on their heels and went slowly towards their own cluster of houses like divines meditating in the sunlight on Galilee or to take up their position under a sacred Indian tree. They provided the one quiet element in an otherwise still noisy village. Women were crying noisily in several houses, giving vent to their nerves. At least one *onjest-mosh* was having hysterics. Somewhere nearby a couple of old men babbled as if they felt their tongues safe to wag in the darkness.

Silk took the woman's hand as they walked on down the street followed by their guards. Her hand no longer shook or expressed agitation but it was seemingly grateful for comfort. When he squeezed it he felt a quick tight pressure in response.

Alas, it did not encourage him. He badly needed someone with whom he could chew things over, mainly to have another opinion on everything which happened here. As things were, she was the last person here in whom he could confide precisely because he still had no positive proof that she had not been put alongside him for precisely that purpose.

Yet he felt fairly sure that his interpretation of the recent incident was correct.

The bald and bearded man had been a genuine junkie. When Silk had regained his wits he saw the puncture-marks inside elbow and knees which proved the man was a main-liner who used a syringe on himself, one from far down Acid Valley. The rest was theory but it added to a total which fitted the event. Someone, a disciple, perhaps two disciples had cut off the junkie's supply and told him he would have to earn it by doing a job for them. He had to attend the dance and pretend it sent him so crazy that he must attack someone, see where the beams of flashlights picked out a man and a woman and rush over and stab the man to death. They must have told the junkie that it would be easy because the man was unarmed. The poor wretch believed them because of his craving, and had not realized that they would kill him because they wanted the Turikrun people to trust them and their fake religion. The superstitious villagers would believe the story because among their legends were many of people being possessed by their version of Satan or one of his aides, and the killing of the junkie would show that Ferdy and his disciples could kill the Devil. And he, Dorian Silk, would be out of the way, unable to pass on information about what happened in the valley, vanished as completely as Bell. Anyone who came in search of him would be told that he had already gone and if they came by helicopter the best thing they could do would be to take off after him. Simple, by golly! It would give Ferdy time to decide what to do.

As they went through a patch of heavy shadow cast by trees the woman leaned sideways from her hips to move her cheek against his shoulder. It was the first gesture she had made since the incident at the dance which gave any indication of her feelings or possible feelings. He put his arm round her waist until they reached the end of the shadow.

Somewhere up in the hills a wolf or wild dog howled. It was a long way off. Down here everything was quiet now that they were out of earshot of the village.

He imagined they were comparatively safe for the present. Since the incident at the dance he included the woman in his own danger, possibly because she might now gain sympathy from her fellow villagers, possibly because she had been told which log they should sit on. He smiled wrily; everything about her came under the heading of 'possibly'. The thought crossed his mind as they walked through another patch of shadow and he took the occasion to put his arm round her again and felt her lithe body react instantly. So he reasoned their safety should last until morning. Ferdy could not act against him again too swiftly or the fear among the villagers uncommitted to his disciples and guards would spread and deepen, worsening Ferdy's position.

Another dog howled up in the hills. It sounded more like a wild dog than a wolf though at this distance his ears might deceive him. He felt Wakhia shudder as she heard it and move closer to him. In another patch of shadow she guided his arm round her and raised his hand to fold on her left breast. No doubt such an action could be wholly sensual in significance, a deception of mood or to conceal involvement in what had happened, but, again possibly, it could have another meaning for her. He felt tension go from her and her body seemed to slacken as if obedient to his need. As things were between them he could see a really nasty moment looming ahead if luck was on his side: sooner or later he would have to decide whether to trust her or not. Perhaps something would happen to resolve the issue.

Throughout the rest of their walk and their return to the village he forced himself to go on thinking. When they climbed the steep steps to the house he was no nearer to solving any of the problems ahead of him. Around them the houses were silent now though he sensed that few people slept. They were lying awake with their worries about what was happening to their once peaceful village, as he was struggling to remember what should fill the holes in his mind and what he had been thinking about when the poor crazed junkie attacked him, some thought which had seemed significant as if he were on the verge of remembering something important. It was significant.

'Ah, damnation,' he whispered two words, as he followed Wakhia into the house.

They found it heavy with stale heat accumulated during the day. With seeming impulsiveness Wakhia drew him across the main room and out onto the balcony to look at the illusion of peacefulness. A yellow radiance from the moon romping across the sky like a Derby winner dimmed all the stars except those low down on the barely visible tops of the hills. The air was thick with the smells of late summer: retained valley heat, grass, trees, night-exhalent bushes, the hint of dust, the skin and hair of the woman beside him. Far away the wolf or wild dog or another howled again. From this point the sound produced a shivery little echo seconds later, sadder, even more eerie. It needed little imagination to guess what legends the Turikrunis like all the isolated valley communities of these hills created from such a weird sound: the lost traveller attacked by a werewolf and doomed to wander throughout history or become a ferocious beast which killed goats and children who strayed too far from home.

He half smiled. That was one of his troubles too and of these people. They could be persuaded to believe almost anything. Including how men disappeared or died.

When the distant creature ceased to howl or went to some place where its misery could not be heard from here the only sound was the yawning grumbling irritated whispers exchanged by the guards below them. There was nothing else. Nothing except the sigh and stir of the woman as he caressed her much to her communicated enjoyment.

After a while she drew him back into the house.

He had expected to stay awake.

Events proved him wrong.

He must have slept deeply for when he awoke he had no recollection of where he was. Then memory came back, limited still working for the enemy. When he looked at his watch it was some time after twelve. They had come to bed less than two hours ago yet he felt completely refreshed, more alert than if he had slept for a night and a day.

Within seconds he found what had awakened him. The woman lay on her side watching him. He could just see that her eyes were wide awake. A cool hand touched him.

In the hills several wolves were noisy now. They were nearer, lower down. Directly one ceased its howl another began, on almost the identical sad note. Perhaps they were one of the reasons why she had lain awake though the urgency of her lips suggested they were not the only one. He found it somewhat difficult to concentrate on whether the wolves were just howling for the hell of it or had been disturbed by something.

No sound reached him from the guards below. Perhaps they were alert, wondering if the far-off howls threatened them. If so, they were mistaken. Wolves seldom if ever attacked humans, unless they were desperate for food for their young and themselves. Most of them were extremely crafty about finding reliable sources of sustenance except in the hazards imposed by winter. Nonetheless, Europeans were frightened of the creatures. No such fear lay against him. After the first fierceness a warmth had come into her and she was relaxed, communicating her needs, shifting at the dictate of want. And this too singled her out, perhaps her womenfolk too, for the women of this region were normally docile in accepting a man rather than a fellow-participator in a celebration. Suddenly a dry sigh came from her throat. Quietness came into her.

Up in the hills the howls went on.

He remained awake for some time. This might be his last chance to think rationally, to even have time to think about what he must do when daylight returned. With two guards at his heels it would be impossible get into the *mandao-jao* to see if Bell was among the dead men there, impossible because at this stage of the game it was unimportant. What was important, truly important, was to get into the armoury and radio centre by creating some diversion, to make sure they were blown, and then to get back to Chitral in case Bell had failed to get there and to ensure that the Pakistani government could get here before either the armoury or the radio house were re-established by Ferdy or whoever followed him here. He doubted if Ferdy would be allowed to remain if his main supply and contact bases were blown. How to do it though? He yawned. First, a little rest, a doze to freshen his mind. He turned on his side and felt his companion move back towards him and grope for his arm to fold it over her. She did not wake.

A sound of angry male voices and running feet awoke him.

He sat up. The sky beyond the balcony of the other room must have the pearl-grey pallor of dawn for he could see the shape of the room and its contents. Although he might regret it later, he ensured his senses came on fully now, alert to every need placed on them. Wakhia too awoke in an instant. He had a glimpse of her strong body and shapely limbs, a tangle of chestnut-coloured hair, wide eyes which turned and hand which reached to him, and then she got swiftly off the bed as he did. She reached for the gown she had thrown across a chair last night as he hauled on his clothes.

Four men burst into the room less than a minute after they finished dressing. Three had automatics in their hands, their eyes searching everything. The fourth man was Hawkins, the one with the quick temper. There was no sign of Hawks.

12

He paused in the act of buttoning his shirt and stared at Hawkins coldly. 'What the devil do you mean by bursting in on us like this?' he demanded. 'I don't mind it. But it's an outrageous insult to this young woman.'

Hawkins glared at him with sick demented eyes. Whether his visible fury was genuine or affected, it had the effect of causing his fat to wobble and he resembled a malevolent garden gnome in a strong wind. He still wore the anaemic flared lilac slacks but the pale blue cotton shirt had been replaced by one of a droopy magnolia tint. In the dim light the face above the Afrikaner fringe-beard had a waxy plumpness. He looked ill in the attic, his eyes full of emotional fury and his lips trembling uncontrollably. His angry laugh sounded like a bark.

'No one can insult these natives,' he snarled. 'They're illiterate animals, most of all their women. Hear me, you stinking cow? I've a bloody good mind to whip you across the floor on your belly, you sow! You, Doctor, if you are a doctor, you don't look like a doctor to me. Where were you an hour ago?

'I don't know what you're talking about.'

'Don't try to hedge! Answer my question! Where were you an hour ago?'

'Here.'

'You were not here!'

'I was here. Asleep until I heard you making a commotion outside.'

'Tell me the truth.' Hawkins stepped towards him like a ballet-dancer. His eyes were very, very sick. 'You know you were not here. You were outside. Away from the village. Don't lie to me, you stinking filth!'

He had quite a line in oldfashioned abuse before four-letter word condemnation became fashionable among top people.

Silk humoured him. 'How could I leave here without you knowing it?' he asked blankly. 'What about the guards Ferdy put on the house?'

Hawkins continued to glare at him while his plump lips massaged each other as if they needed regular loving care. 'They went to sleep,' he gritted eventually. The words sounded as if they were dragged out of him by a juggernaut lorry. 'They don't remember when they fell asleep. And you took advantage of them.'

'Is it a crime to fall asleep?'

'It is when you go out and stab one of our believers to death while he's on duty down the valley!'

Silk absorbed the information and its implications while they looked at each other. Hawkins's eyes were probing him to find a weakness. Silk gave a disbelieving smile and shook his head incredulously.

The eyes of Hawkins wanted him dead right then. The automatic waved menacingly, 'The death of one of our followers is nothing to smirk about, you bloody fraud!' he yelled, and went silent as they heard the sound of a helicopter flying up the valley towards the village. A triumphant leer spread wide across Hawkins's face. 'Now we shall have some order here!' he enthused. 'Not before time. You – whoever you are – you'd better confess you killed our friend. We can make sure you tell us the truth. No one can destroy the peace of our Fourth Heaven and live!'

Silk shook his head again in disbelief as everyone except the woman stared at him. Although Hawkins was in a highly emotional state the other men were in full control of themselves. And of their automatics, though they were under the authority of Hawkins or so it seemed.

'I'll wait until Ferdy or Mr Hawks can get here,' Silk said as if pacifying an excitable child. 'You are clearly distraught.'

'A doctor! I told them you're no doctor!'

There was no means of telling whether or not this was another tricky attempt to get rid of him.

'You may recall I told your friends I am not a medical doctor,' Silk said, his voice rising against the approaching clatter; later he would try to decide about its significance, now he merely noted that it came from the direction of Afghanistan. 'Have you asked the guards if they came up here to find out if I was absent – after they awoke? Did you even ask them? Or did you come here and find them asleep and assume that I was out? If so, why am I here?' He pushed authority into his voice as he looked at each man in turn. 'Were any of these men involved? I suppose one or two of them must have been.'

'Yes no?' Hawkins shouted. He was trembling, his voice thick as if he were on the verge of tears. It made him far more dangerous than he was at their earlier encounter. Every sign told that it would not take much to goad him into really rash action and none of the other men looked likely to dissuade him; they belonged to the huge ranks of those who accepted casual violence as a norm and a release for the unsatisfied animal inside them; you saw their type on television screens every time there was a demo. They would just watch and giggle at anything which happened.

Silk tried to play for time. 'You'd better tell me what that means,' he said.

They were all silent as the helicopter clattered deafeningly low overhead. It sank into view beyond the balcony as the pilot landed it somewhere just beyond the houses. As the noise lessened to a point where speech became possible again, Silk went on: 'You have three of your brothers here. I don't know them, I don't know any of them except those who have been introduced to me. If you do anything violent each of these men will remember I have denied and do deny having left this house since I brought Wakhia back from the dance. They will be able to tell Ferdy and anyone else what I said when you accused me.'

A bully, Hawkins loathed being forced into a corner. 'You're lying!' he yelled wildly.

'Why should I? Why do you want to believe I'm lying? Why me? You seem determined to make sure I'm lying. God knows why. Ask this young woman if I left the house.'

Hawkins sneered voluptuously and gave a general condemnation of women and their part in life. 'What's the use of asking the poor bitch anything?' he asked contemptuously. 'She would lie to save you.' He went off on another flight of abuse. Then he snarled: 'She's only an illiterate native, a savage. She thinks she owes you a debt for making her body feel good for a couple of nights.' He laughed cynically. 'Woman are like that. Fool around with them and they're like dogs.'

He glared at Silk, eager for him to do a nineteenth-century hero act and leap to the physical defence of a woman, which would give him and his brothers an excuse to use their guns.

'Tell me,' Silk said mildly, 'are your views about women shared by all the members of the Fourth Heaven? Is that what you called it? The Fourth Heaven? There are so many new religions about nowadays it's tricky to keep count of their number if you have a memory like mine. Actually, from what Ferdy and Mr Hawks told me, I thought you welcomed these women into your community and intended to establish them as full members. After all, we're all natives of somewhere. Even you. And I am indebted to this young woman, not she to me. I'm sure she and all the other women here who have joined your community believe what Ferdy told me, not what you've just said about her and all women.'

He had talked straight through a succession of yelps and shouts from Hawkins and several menacing waves of the automatic. Now he ended of his own accord, watching the enraged little man. Hawkins had lost some steam. For the first time since he and his companions burst into the room he looked at them and evidently he saw some doubt in their faces. He chose to ignore it.

'You're getting too bloody careless!' he warned, his voice rising more and more shrilly, eyes glittering. 'I'll make you confess you killed my friend or I'll kill you!'

'Your friend?' Silk queried gently, 'What sort of friend, Mr Hawkins?'

The man opened his mouth to yell something. Then he stopped, mouth still open, his face looking as if it had just run headlong into a stationary bus without seeing it. Abruptly his lips went back to massaging each other for consolation. For a moment he looked on the verge of breaking down, his face sunk like poor pastry. He opened his mouth and snapped it shut again. Silk had a feeling that the man's blind fury was draining out of him and left him with nothing. It might be that he was enduring the worst part of the only really human emotion he had ever known, and, without it, was bereft. His gaze went from Silk to the floor.

Silk chose his next words and their tone carefully. It was easier now that the helicopter had landed and shut off its engine. There was a chance, no more than a thin one, that this might not be another put-up job, but an explosion of genuine emotional imbalance which sought expression and picked on the one individual at the great disadvantage. It stood to reason that Hawkins would not pick a quarrel with his 'brothers', the disciples and guards here who would bear it against him as a grudge. And Hawkins knew it would be dangerous to bully a villager without reason. Once roused, the people could make it awkward for their present rulers.

'I didn't know your friend,' Silk said expressionlessly. 'I had no cause to kill him or kill anyone here. Everyone here except my friend Bell, is a complete stranger to me. I have been in this house all night. You say he was killed with a dagger – no, you said he was stabbed to death. I have no dagger.'

'We may find it in the house!'

Silk sat down on the bed and pulled Wakhia down beside him. 'I'm not responsible if you've brought one with you and hidden it somewhere,' he said coldly, and looked aside.

The men with Hawkins made a thorough search. Silk and the woman stood while they examined the bed and then sat down again until they were frisked; the brother who searched her showed no inclination to hurry. No likely hiding-place was left untouched. Two of the men obviously knew how the Turikrunis hid their cherished possessions; that suggested they were lovers of deserted women. Silk watched them open the board where the woman had put the revolver and ammunition.

The cavity was empty.

He sat still waiting for the men to finish. At no time did he look at the woman though questions about what had happened to the things she hid went through his mind. If she had started on a plan of her own it would add new complications which he would sooner avoid. She was motionless, head lowered, hands folded on lap. No hint of nervousness agitated her limp fingers. She ignored him as steadily as he ignored her.

After a quarter of an hour the men admitted defeat. Not so Hawkins. He had committed himself too far to give in. While the search was in progress he had regained part of his earlier rage. When it ended he stalked across the room and stood in front of Silk and swiped him twice across the mouth like an old-time movie toughie delivering the final insult to another's manhood. Silk did not respond. Years ago he had learned to quell his natural tendency to be provoked except on his own terms. Hawkins loosed a string of oaths at him and the woman. She probably did not understand them. Silk did. He did absolutely nothing, ignoring the voice with its schoolboy abuse in a variety of languages. When Hawkins ran out of that ploy he drew several deep breaths while he thought up a variation. It did not take him long.

'You think you're bloody clever, don't you, you crafty sly coward?' he gritted. 'I know you killed Jerzy and I'm going to prove it.' He slapped Silk's face again and spat at him. Enraged, he thrust the automatic into the waistband of his trousers and grabbed Silk's neck in his plump hands.

A voice came from the doorway. 'What's going on here?' Hawks demanded furiously. 'Stop behaving like a fool! Let Doctor Eden go and tell me what this is about.'

Hawkins spun round to face him and launched into a long explanation which told nobody anything. Silk noted that it was in fluent German with the sort of vowels you heard in Hamburg and Lubeck although his earlier English had been so accentless that it was flavourless. Hawks kept silent, standing still, hands thrust deep into the pockets of his khaki-coloured safari jacket, a genuine article instead of the tatty rubbish invented by the rag trade for suburbia, his eyes very busy as they studied the woman, stared penetratively at the three guards, glanced once at Silk, and then let his gaze go round the room while he listened. The three guards became more uneasy with every passing second; their faces showed they clearly wished to be somewhere else. Silk knew he had no reason to cheer at the reprieve; it merely meant that Hawkins had acted on his own initiative and thereby had embarrassed Ferdy and Hawks who preferred to kill off suspect visitors by methods which could be claimed as quite accidental. Still, it was temporarily encouraging to see that Hawks now had an authority nowhere apparent in the emotional and jabbering Hawkins. When the sad tirade ended with another crescendo of abuse Hawks looked at Silk again.

'Did you leave the house during the night, Doctor?' he asked.
'No.'

'Our brother is convinced you took advantage of the

guards being asleep, to slip out unseen.'

'Your brother talks a lot of damfool nonsense.'

'You hear him, you hear?' Hawkins raved.

'Be quiet,' Hawks told him. 'Can you prove you didn't leave it, Doctor?'

'No.'

'You sound sure.'

'I am. He told me I couldn't prove I stayed here and that this woman would lie that I remained in the house because, according to him, she owes me some form of debt and is only an illiterate savage who no normal man would befriend.'

'He's lying! He's . . .'

'Wait,' Hawks said and brought his hands from his pockets and put them behind his back. He looked at the guards. 'Is that what Brother Hawkins said?'

None of them answered. They were busy, looking elsewhere. Hawks turned to Silk again.

'What have you to say, Doctor?'

'Who will listen to me?'

'I will.'

'Very well,' Silk said aggrievedly. 'The whole of Mr Hawkins's argument is stupid. Daft. He has a habit of working himself into a state of high excitability and then believing whatever he wants to believe. It is thoroughly illogical and unscientific. True, we have quite a number of scientists who behave similarly if they dwell too long on a particular theory and want everyone to believe it is a basic or fundamental truth. One expected more sanity among the members of this admirable community.' He paused. 'Do you want me to say why Mr Hawkins's reasoning is childish?'

'Give me some reasons,' Hawks said, nodding.

'To begin with, Mr Hawkins has not said why I should leave here during the night. He has not given a reason why I should wait up, popping in and out to see if the guards were asleep until they were. Whenever that was. He has not said why, after my experience last evening, I should choose to go down the valley alone when the guards had given me and this young woman protection earlier on. I suppose it is possible to obtain a dagger here. I have not done so. He has not said why I should want one. He has not even said why I should stab to death somebody or other who was a friend of his and then come back here. Or how the guards happened to be still asleep when I arrived. Or what I did with the dagger.'

Silk stopped. He drew a breath. 'You will have seen other things,' he said. 'But really the whole of his accusations are too trivial and absurd.'

'Did you point these things out to him?'

'He was too busy shouting and raving for me to be able to reason with him.'

Hawkins nodded. A slight smile hovered around his lips and he ignored the incoherent fulminations coming from the crazed man, gazing first at one of them and then at the other. 'You are quite right, Doctor,' he agreed in a most friendly manner. 'He has been most annoying to you. And your woman friend. I apologise on behalf of us all.' He turned to Hawkins. 'Your unhappiness led you to act stupidly,' he said in a tight voice, trying to conceal anger by masking it with reproof. 'Doctor Eden is our honoured guest. Go away and come back and apologise to him later. We . . .'

Hawkins interrupted. For the last few minutes his lips had twitched up and down over each other in a frenzied manner. Now his inner fury boiled over again. In an ecstasy of German compounds he accused everyone in the room of being insane and more. He glared wildly at Hawks.

'I have endured your insults too long!' he raved. 'You have always tried to abuse me in front of the brothers! You spread lies about me!'

He sounded close to tears but kept on, ignoring repeated orders by Hawks to get control of himself and remember where he was. Silk felt as uneasy as if he was sitting in on a family row. The only person who had paid no attention to the argument was the woman. Once she had lifted her head to look at Silk as if to reassure him about something. Then she looked down again. Her hands remained quiet on her lap.

Hawkins sucked air into his lungs. 'Now that Nicholas has come I intend to tell him about you!' he shouted. 'And about Ferdy! You are a traitor. He is inefficient.'

'Go away and calm down,' Hawks ordered sharply.

Hawkins gave no sign of hearing. He had a remarkable ability to hear only his own voice or its echoes going round inside his head. His face changed as he stared at Hawks, his eyes filling with hatred.

'Traitors should die,' he said savagely and levelled his automatic at Hawks.

The noise was deafening. Although Hawkins pulled the trigger of his gun it could only have been a muscular spasm and the bullet flew into the roof. He was already dead. A bullet from the automatic Hawks had produced from behind his back, and which must have been in his pocket, had smashed into the other man's forehead, jerking him back off his feet and tossing him onto the floor. His feet twitched as if tightened by cramp.

Too late, everyone had clapped their hands over their ears. Silk winced as the double explosion clapped thunderously on his ears and went on ringing excruciatingly through his head. The woman was swaying from side to side, hands over ears, body shuddering. A guard with a stunned face walked forward mechanically, stepping over the body, shaking his head continually as he blundered to the opposite wall, turned, and came back. His legs seemed weak.

Hawks showed no visible reaction. He merely gazed at the body of Hawkins as if he was looking at fish on a slab. After some seconds he inspected his automatic, grimaced at the smell, and waved it about like a woman trying to lose the peardrop odour of her nail varnish. The guard twisted his head as if in agony. After some minutes the woman touched Silk's thigh and then her hand fell listlessly into her lap.

Silk waited until he could hear and be heard. His opinion of those who lead the community of brothers had sunk even lower. None of them were intelligent, merely dangerous. He glowered at Hawks.

'Was that necessary?' he demanded angrily. 'You may have permanently damaged the hearing of one or more of us!'

As Hawks pocketed the automatic with a businesslike flourish there was a thunderous explosion. It came from farther down the valley but the absence of barriers except the strips of woodland lent it an illusion of being much closer. Silk saw the guards look at each other and then at him. So did Hawks. Simultaneously with the shock wave hitting the house so that it trembled around them and the men had difficulty in keeping their balance there was another explosion. The first had been a deep heavy *boooom*! This was sharper, more vicious, like a rattle of automatic-fire after the detonation of a heavy gun. Within a split second the wave hit them. It came stronger. The whole house seemed to sway. One man dropped to his knees.

No true silence followed. All through the village voices started to call, women full of alarm, men fierce with anger, small girls wailing, the *onjest-mosh* querulous and panicky. As Hawks led the race out onto the balcony there was a third explosion. It resembled the first but was smaller, lazier. Silk ignored the levelled automatics to follow Hawks.

They saw at least three separate columns of smoke knitting into a single billowing grey-brown plume which rose above the two buildings which stood by by themselves. Silk knew what had happened. So did Hawks, cursing furiously to himself as he saw an orange-red glow circle the bases of the houses and flames lick up through the smoke. Most of the smoke now was thick oily brown. Other smaller explosions continued, an occasional boom like a clumsy hand-clap with hollowed palms, an almost continuous rattle which at this distance sounded like thousands of Chinese crackers going off, the chatter of exploding small-arms ammunition in the heat. Silk saw a small piece of blazing timber dart away from the right side of the nearest building. Except that it was not a piece of timber; it was a man on fire. They saw him blunder around already too far gone to know what he did until finally he fell. Within seconds another man came out of the blaze, running until he tripped over something and pitched into a pile of wood and set it alight.

Silk did not need anyone to tell him that he had indeed had an extremely lucky escape. If he had left the woman, as Hawkins had believed, he might have been in one or other of the houses as they blew. The thought, the sense of relief it brought, was academic. What counted was that Bell had succeeded. By means known only to himself, he had got into each building in turn and used all his skill to fuse them to go off at this particular hour. Perhaps no one would ever know precisely why he rigged them to go off at this particular hour. It might be that he had not expected Silk to come and had rigged them for a time when no one else would consider such a possibility at all likely. He might have thought that Silk would come and had prepared the charges for an hour when he knew him unlikely to be anywhere near them. The second explosion coming so soon after the first proved that it was hardly likely to have been accidental. That was possible but unlikely. The reason might be something completely different, a psychological gambit. What else?

The helicopter?

Why?

What connexion could it have with the blow? And how was the man mentioned by Hawkins only a few moments ago . . . what was his name? Nicholas? Had the helicopter brought him?

Silk found no singular hardship over appearing bewildered. He was. Something in his temperament rejected the mere idea of such a rush of dramatic events before he had even had a cup of tea to revive, if possible, his jaded brain. Particularly after . . . no matter at present.

He had a recollection that Bell's elder brother had been a sabotage expert in explosives during World War Two who dropped into France on several missions. Perhaps it was his father or an uncle, but he had some relative who fell to help the Maquis blow ammunition trains and goods-yards, factories and power-plants, which the RAF had some bother in locating from above. Which relation it was would be proud of Bell's handiwork here. The houses would burn until they were empty blackened shells.

As he waited for Hawks to speak or do something he felt the woman's body come against his back. Perhaps she knew the reason for what had happened though she would not have been told; this was not the sort of information a genuinely professional agent passed to anyone.

Village voices were all round them. Silk saw the first guards and disciples running down towards the blazing houses; they were too late. A struggle of children flew after them. Somewhere in the street a woman started to keen the death threnody uttered by the women of such communities; perhaps her guard-lover was among the possible dead and she knew it.

A glance at Hawks' bearded profile told Silk nothing. The beard provided a good disguise. But his immobility betrayed him. He was too stunned, too unbelieving, to have a clear idea of what to do or whether it was worth doing. It might well be that he saw the fires destroying the result of months of careful preparation.

Well, it depended on how deeply you believed in what you believed. Silk did not believe the views now being so assiduously spread everywhere by Coms masquerading as pacifists that the rest of the world should disarm while Kremlin Coms put their strutting iron-clad army on it droning clatter every year through Red Square around noon and their vastly bemed-alled Genghis Khan-type marshals praised the magnificence of

Soviet arms. He never would believe it. His own pet little homily was that there was no point in saving the world from Hitler merely to hand it over the Stalin's heirs. Consequently he never fell for the argument that the American President had no right to disregard the wishes of Congress but the President of Chile, a Com, had every right to disregard the wishes of his government; nor did he accept the strange propaganda yarns hawked around the world by turbulent young priests out of Africa about White beastliness there which prevented them from condemning Black beastliness. And here, however deeply Hawks might believe in his Com views, well, why not say they were Com and let them prove themselves without this fanciful religious hocus-pocus? The Com mind was a very queer instrument. It had the devious emotionalism of abnormal psychology.

Hawks coughed sharply. Silk turned towards him. The man was watching him with baleful eyes. His manner had undergone a profound change. Here we go again, Silk told himself.

'So!' Hawks said and blew heavily down his nose. 'Perhaps my colleague was right. You did leave here during the night.'

Silk did not intend to play the game. 'What the devil do you mean?' he snapped indignantly. 'Mr Hawks, I'm becoming extremely tired of this extraordinary behaviour! What is going on here? First of all that man accuses me of leaving here and you recognised the stupidity of his accusation. Then you shoot him. Now you repeat his accusation. What is going on?'

The glossy beard rippled. The eyes above it had narrowed, showed rage and fear. 'You were very clever,' Hawks said, thickly. 'You deceived me completely.'

'Deceived you? What do you mean?'

'You know very well.'

'I do not know. The sooner my friends come and take me away from here the better. This is all extremely unlike the courtesy usually shown to a traveller.'

'You did leave the house during the night,' Hawks stated emphatically.

'Don't be absurd! Do you speak this woman's language? Ask her!'

Hawks jerked his head towards the street below. 'Do you hear that woman screaming?' he asked. 'None of these women like to lose a man. She has just lost one.'

Silk drew a long breath and exhaled slowly. 'What has that to do with it?' he asked tiredly.

'Any of these women will do anything to keep a man if she gets one.'

'That is still not unusual in some societies.'

'I mean, this one would lie in order to keep you.'

Silk gazed at him incredulously. 'When you and everyone here knows I shall be leaving this evening or early tomorrow morning?' he asked, and laughed incredulously. 'How can she "lie in order to keep" me here? What has this to do with the friend of Mr Hawkins who was killed?'

'He was one of our fraternity. He was on guard outside the village. At the approach to those houses.'

'Oh. Are they sacred houses to these people or your brother-hood or fraternity or whatever you call it?'

Another woman had started to keen while they talked, shrilling her grief into the early sunlight. It consisted of a single high-pitched note which broke and then soared and fell like the Spanish *saeta* cried by women on street balconies at the penitential parades during Eastertide. As the wail went on Hawks took the automatic from his pocket again. It did not threaten. It merely warned.

'Well?' Silk demanded, even more truculently. He had plenty of patience to maintain his role, indeed he could not do anything else, but he was fast running out of ideas on how to keep on handling the same situation with different men in the character. Another thought had occurred to rob him of some confidence. It might have been Bell who knifed Hawkins's boy friend last night in order to enter the houses and set the fuses. If so, either he might be one of the running flames whom they had seen or had died inside one house as it blew. In a moment of crisis he could only increase the authority of the part he played as any ordinary man who stumbled into this situation would do, regardless of the consequences. 'Well?' he shouted.

For the second time in the past half hour assistance came from an unexpected source.

'What is the matter?' asked an unfamiliar voice behind them, a voice so knowledgeable of its authority that it did not need to shout or bluster.

They turned. In the shadows beyond the opening to the room were two men. One was Ferdy. The other was a tall thin man in a travel-crumpled pale grey suit. He had a bronzed goodlooking sort of face, the features lean and clad in a pleasantly unemphatically ascetic sort of style, and his sleekly curled grey hair was absurdly short by modern standards. He was probably in his early forties but looked several years older, and very fit. He could have been anything from the financial adviser of an international company who enjoyed his art collection and good wine to a man down on his luck who believed in keeping up appearances. His wide-lipped mouth had an atmosphere of being about to smile at any time.

'Who are you?' Silk demanded irately. He judged this manifestation no reason to change his role. 'What is happening? Is that you, Ferdy?'

'This is the Superior Brother of our Fourth Kingdom,' Ferdy said in a reverential tone. 'Brother Nicholas. He organises our contacts with those in the world outside who come to seek our faith.'

'Oh, he does, does he?' Silk said agrily. 'Then perhaps he can tell me why a drug addict tries to kill me, why that man Hawkins rushed in accusing me of murder, Mr Hawks here first defended me – to the point of killing Hawkins quite needlessly – and then charges me with the same crimes that Hawkins accused me of earlier. What in Heaven's name is going on here?'

He used his voice to imply bewilderment and irritation and indignation and to state a conviction in ultimate personal safety for which he had absolutely no justification.

'I suggest we get rid of these people and talk about it,' Nicholas said. His voice matched his hair beautifully. 'Mr Hawks, you will take these men away while Ferdy and I talk to Doctor Eden.'

They talked for nearly an hour. During that time Silk realised he did not know whether the radio-station house had blown before Ferdy had learned his identity from 'our little friend' in Islamabad, but he acted on the assumption that he had no alternative except to go on playing the same role and hope that he did not commit himself into making errors. He had also gained respect for Nicholas. The newcomer was a very cool and unemotional character; a perfect type to establish a network and control it. He was the sort of man who read poetry if he got caught in a traffic jam during the rush hour. Not that they had traffic jams in Moscow. His accent was pure Muscovite.

At the conclusion of the interview Nicholas stood up smiling and said: 'Leave it to Ferdy and me, Doctor Eden. You had better stay safely in here with our sister until your friends arrive later today or tomorrow. These people are very superstitious and may become violent if they associate you with the various tragedies which have happened because you came here.'

That was his first error. It came like the telegraphed warning of an old boxer. The visitor no one had wanted to enter the valley must now remain a prisoner in one of its houses. Silk frowned.

'This young woman and I have certain human requirements,' he commented.

'Of course,' Nicholas agreed sympathetically. 'We will increase the guard to protect you. Four men, I think, Ferdy?'

He took Ferdy away. As their voices faded down the alley between the houses the woman came across the room from where she had been standing silent throughout the entire interview and put her hand in his. Her eyes were worried but tried to give him encouragement. Although he smiled she did not succeed. He knew when he was in a cage like an old-time con on Death Row waiting for execution.

13

After they got back from their walk to the nearest wood which had a stream of icy mountain water running through it in which they could freshen their faces and set their skins tingling, they were left alone except for the anonymous guards at the steps outside.

Directly they went in they saw that the body of Hawkins had gone. Attempts had been made to remove the bloodstains. Only a couple of flies were curious. After Wakhia got breakfast and they finished the meal he sat out on the balcony trying to think ahead and to remember. He got no joy.

All through the morning village women and the few men who had not joined the trek to a more profitable area went to look at the wrecked buildings. Occasional dribbles of smoke came from the ruins. Two women stayed at the scene on their knees and beating their chests. A group of boy virgins hovered nearby to watch guards search the ruins.

Shortly before noon a funeral procession of lamenting women and silent men left the village behind a coffin borne shoulder-high by guards. It stopped outside the *jestak-kan* where a white-haired *rebun*, probably the chief *pshé*, emerged to cry out exhortations to assist the occupant of the box on its next stage of the journey.

Silk was always conscious of the guards muttering worriedly below.

All morning the disciples were conspicuous by their

absence. It was presumably a tactic not to antagonise local people or to keep them out of sight until a decision had been taken on how to explain recent events.

They had their midday meal out on the balcony. He stayed on there alone after she had retreated into the house. Still no really reliable plan came to him.

The afternoon became sultry and the air had a thundery heaviness. He went into the bedroom and lay down there, naked to the waist, afraid lest one of the gigantic thunderstorms which frequently raged around these hills should hamper his inevitable attempt to escape. He saw that the woman too could not settle. At first she tried to twine her hair into plaits but within minutes she undid them impatiently as if they gave her a headache. She started a slow aimless prowl around the rooms. At her third or fourth reappearance he spoke her name.

At once she changed her direction and came across and sat down on the space he cleared for her. The hand he took had moisture in its palm, a residue of strain quivering in the fingers. He began to caress her. After some moments they stood up and undressed. She came into his arms directly they lay down, eager to make love and forget whatever troubled her.

Around them the afternoon retained its heat. Occasionally they were aware of voices but none came near. No one bothered them.

When they got up to dress his head had lost the drowsiness which bothered it after lunch. Both of them had fallen asleep at times. Under his touch her skin was cooler and he saw that her eyes were easier than they had been since yesterday afternoon. She indicated pleasure at the movement of his hand over her shoulders and clung to him for a moment. Then some modesty took her into the other room to dress by herself.

A glance at his watch showed he had less than three hours in which to decide what to do. Frowning, he belted his trousers and decided there was no longer any use in trying to remember the nameless 'little friend' and his woman in Rawalpindi. The time for such exercises had long passed. So had the need to prowl round the *mandao-jao* and to worry about the houses which Bell had blown by some means. His sole need now was to decide how to leave here and when to go, in order to ensure that news of what had happened and was happening here reached those who should be told and in case Bell had failed to get away. He wondered if he should do anything about the helicopter sitting silently down there just outside the village. It was some time since he had last flown a whirlybird, but the problem now was whether he could get past the guards who must be protecting it and take off without being shot down like the one on the hillside. After some minutes he decided against it. The risks were too great. He had to go on his feet.

'Oh, easy,' he muttered.

Belatedly a thought which should have come to his over-busy, addled mind hours ago flew through it like a bird. He cursed his stupidity. Nothing excused it. It should have been attended to hours ago, directly after Nicholas and Ferdy had left the house. He strode into the next room and found the woman coiling a necklace above her gown.

As she smiled a welcome he asked tensely: 'Where did you hide the revolver and ammunition? I thought they were in the compartment.'

Smiling more freely, she shook her head. She took his hand and led him back into the other room and pointed to a beam which crossed the room above the bed. It was not more than ten inches wide. It gave him a sick sensation in the stomach to realise that if the explosions at the two houses had been any louder they would easily have shaken off the weapon and the box of bullets, and then everything would have been all up for both of them. He had read of people breaking into a cold sweat; maybe he didn't but it felt damn near to it. He looked at Wakhia again and saw she was still smiling, obviously very pleased with herself.

'Clever girl,' he said quietly, and saw her eyes gleam. 'And beautiful too.'

She understood the compliment and it confused her. Yet it was true. In the half-light and despite the lingering heat she appeared remarkably fresh and unbothered for a woman living through tumultuous hours whichever side she served. And love-making did for her what it did for other fortunate women; it sharpened awareness of a strong and shapely female entity into something more positively memorable. She half-closed her eyes as he moved her shoulder in his hand.

'Tell me,' he said in the same quiet voice, 'have you got a dagger?'

At once her forehead dipped briefly and she turned and ran from the room. Within a minute she brought it to him; she must have hidden that somewhere too for it was precisely the sort of weapon which would have led Hawkins to condemn him without listening to any argument. It was in a dark leather sheath and was fairly small, the straight blade not much more than six inches long, if that, but both cutting edges were sharp. He hefted it experimentally and found its balance better than he expected. It could have come from anywhere, Birmingham or Banaras, Sheffield or Simla. The chief thing was it could be used. She watched while he tried a few practice flips at a knot of wood in one wall and found he could still use such a weapon fairly well if he had to. He put it back into its sheath.

Partly reassured, he paced round the room thinking, motioning her to stay as he turned towards the other room, and finally went back to her. 'I must leave here and go back to my friends,' he told her.

Momentarily her face lost its self-control. He saw a muscle tighten at the corners of her lips. She waited, watching him.

'It will be dangerous,' he said in the same lowered voice. 'You understand, don't you? Yes, I thought you did. The men here will try to stop me from going. They will stop my friends from meeting me here.' That was the only sentence he included to intentionally confuse her. 'So I must go soon. If they find I have gone they will follow me and I think they will try to kill me. But I must go because these men can only bring unhappiness to your people.' He doubted if that meant much to her as a woman who had been shunned by her own menfolk but tribal loyalties sometimes went deeper than personal bitterness; beside, every woman alive was a professional survivor. 'Will you stay here or do you want to come with me?'

He knew as he asked her that the question put his head fairly on the block. If she had a voice this was the minute, the exact second, when she should yell at the top of her breath and bring everyone within hearing distance thundering up the steps to listen to her public denunciation and accusation. There was absolutely nothing he could do if she once got started on a long deep breath.

Her eyes asked questions. Even if he knew what they were, he could not answer them with any degree of assurance. His stomach still felt peculiar from the knowledge of discovering one vital point, the location of the revolver, which had completely gone from his mind. Usually he was always full of such items in a hour of some confusion and threat. If he forgot that, what else might he forget or not see clearly or interpret accurately on a dash away from the village? He gave her a big waiting smile.

She turned her back to him. Cold again, he waited for the scream. It did not come. After a moment she faced him again though her gaze went everywhere while she thought, a frown between her brows. It took several long minutes. At length, not too surely, her hand found his. After a few seconds her grip tightened. Her gaze sought his. She nodded.

'Good,' he said. 'You're brave. We'll go directly it gets dark. We'd better have some food now. And have you something we can take with us?'

At the approach of night the village seemed to have a

brooding atmosphere as if its people waited for a storm to erupt. When he stood on the balcony there was nobody in sight. He heard only the whimper of a fretful child. A curl of smoke came from one of the blown houses down the valley.

A touch on his arm drew him back into the house. The woman had prepared a substantial though not sleep-enducing meal. As they finished it he put his hand on her shoulder to gain attention.

'Are you sure you want to come?' he asked.

She nodded casually as if the question had never given her any misgiving.

He turned his head to glance out across the verandah. The sky was losing light faster. No sound reached him. That was odd. He could not hear the guards. His mind suddenly reminded him that he had not heard them when he stood on the verandah while Wakhai prepared their meal.

He could guess what was about to happen. Everyone was taking decisions. He turned to Wakhia. 'Go and see if the guards are down there,' he said, and needed no one to tell him the risk he ran. 'Don't take any chances.'

Without hesitation she stood up and left the room.

In her absence he went into the other room and climbed onto the bed to collect the revolver and ammunition.

As he stepped off the bed she came into the room. She shook her head, her eyes wide with surprise and spread her hands. That confirmed his fears.

'No one?' he queried, almost hoping there might be one guard below.

She shook her head.

So that proved it. They had planned something, some event, something to happen soon, when the villagers were in their homes waiting for the evening meal. Nicholas or Ferdy had realised they had no alternative except to take some action which might serve to prop up the dwindling impact of their fake religion with disciples, its Fourth Heaven, its drug addicts and men in need of women – no ashram this – its guards and guns and weapons. They knew the villagers were not the stupid ignorant fools they had supposed and were becoming dubious of their supposed saviours. That meant that he and the woman were once again cast as the sacrificial lambs in some impending event.

'We have to go now,' he said abruptly. 'You get the food.'

Three minutes later they crept cautiously down the narrow steps. The woman was right. The guards had been withdrawn.

14

Scarcely any light showed among the tight clusters of houses. Hardly any voices engaged in conversation; it would have been natural to hear some exchanges in ordinary Turikruni houses and the European disciples and guards must have evolved some basic communication with their women. But the only voices to be heard were an old man and an old woman muttering disconsolately and three boys whispering in a dark alley.

The silence did not help. Every step seemed to sound. At one point Silk could almost believe he heard himself breath.

He led the woman forward down narrow alleys between the houses and paused at each corner and in every pool of shadow. Uncertainty plagued him. He had decided, a long time ago it seemed now, to leave by the route which brought him here, rather than waste energy and time on any other, but every minute his choice seemed more hazardous. They could come face to face with a patrol of armed guards.

Behind him Wakhia kept close. She acted intelligently; occasionally a slight touch of her hand on his waist told him she was there but made no demands. One part of his attention fastened on her automatically, part of the task in hand in case his hopes about her should prove unfounded in the final testing. Once in a while the basket in which she carried their food and extra ammunition brushed against his legs.

They had crept down past four houses when he saw why the guards who had been on duty outside the woman's house were withdrawn. This was the only way to reach the house from the village street, as he had noted on earlier occasions. As they rounded one corner he saw a man coming towards him. He placed the man instantly; he was one of the group of junkies which shambled onto the clearing to watch the dance last evening. Either that or he was one of the disciples or guards pretending to be a junkie. His walk, the quivering smile on his dazed face, his limp arms and hands, the occasional soft giggle, suggested he was either drunk or in the first stage of a trip. There was no method by which they could avoid him.

Silk knew that he had anonymity for only a few moments if the man tried to pick a quarrel with anyone who passed him. He reached behind for the woman's hand and drew her forward in front of him. No hesitation came from her. As she walked towards the man Silk kept close to her and lowered his head.

They were almost past the man and Silk had begun to feel they might get away with it when the man decided to take a closer look at them. He gave a giggle and reached out a long arm to grab hold of Silk and swing him round. Silk raised his head. For a moment they stared straight at one another. The man was clearly disconcerted, as well he might be. He was no hippie, though he wore hippie-style clothes and had tarted his face up to resemble a hippy revolt against suburbia. His disconcertation undid him somewhat. It telegraphed his attention, the quick movement of his right hand towards the waistband of his trousers, the way his mouth opened to attract attention by a yell for help. Instead he gave a short breathly squawk like an offended hen as the side of Silk's hand struck the side of his neck a fierce blow. The man fell sideways, his knees gone and the gun for which he reached fell out of his trousers. Silk caught him as he sagged and spun him around, and finished the job. It only took seconds. Silk saw no valid reason to have a long discussion with his conscience about how to deal with a man who intended to kill him and probably the woman.

Quickly he dragged the mortal remains into the space under the nearest house where the people kept their goats. None were there now but he found a pile of sacks and covered the dead man. When he went back into the alley Wakhia gave him the automatic which the man had carried. The feel of it told him it had a full clip inside. She laid a hand on his arm as if to reassure him about something and then stood back.

They went on down between the silent houses fading into darkness.

Near the street he went more slowly. They could not have left the house more than ten, maybe twelve minutes ago, though every minute felt like an hour and each second had acquired a remarkable longevity. Yet still the silence continued, strange, unnatural, in his ears.

He had a conviction that the entire village was hushed while it waited for something to happen. What? He had no idea. It could easily be that the true villagers had become so used to dramatic events in the last forty-eight hours that they automatically expected something else to happen, like people who were accident prone or towns under enemy air-raids, a communicated conviction of impending disaster. It could be more than that though he had no means to tell what it might be.

He chewed his underlip and listened intently.

At a division where two alleys crossed at right angles he halted unsurely. The path ahead led straight on between houses which fronted onto the street: once there they would be out in the open and about half a mile, maybe more, from the route up to the pass. If possible he wanted to reach the crest of the pass, bound to be guarded as it was when he arrived, before the shooting started. Clearly the left-hand alley was out: if it led anywhere it would only head them down the valley. The right-hand section twisted away into shadows between dilapidated old farm buildings and equally old houses. It might be a cul-de-sac. It could lead straight to another derelict house.

The woman decided for them. Her cold hand took hold of

his and drew him down the right-hand path. She had obviously interpreted his dilemma . . . he hoped.

Darkness made the first section of the winding alley tricky for a stranger. At times he only knew Wakhia was there because her hand drew him forward. He did not see her until the alley widened enough to admit the last light from the sky.

They passed a house where a baby cried. Otherwise the silence continued and seemed to harden, though that could easily be a trick of his own nerves. At least he knew why Nicholas and Ferdy and their men were silent. They were waiting for a sound of shots which would shatter the stillness. Perspiration trickled down behind his ears. It had been a trifle too close.

A minute later they reached the end of the buildings.

The woman took her cue from observing how he had worked their course so far. She led them into the last patch of shadow to let him decide what to do. He gripped her shoulder with his free hand and whispered 'Thank you' and she touched his side.

He looked around.

They had reached the limit of the village and of the valley. Ahead of them beyond a strip of bare ground about a hundred yards across was the wood he remembered climbing the steeply sloping ground on this side of the pass, at present an inky blob without benefit of moonlight. The path to the pass itself must be several hundred yards away on the left as he looked at the wood now.

His lips found the woman's ear. 'Is there only one pass on this side?' he whispered, and felt her hair glide down against his face as she dipped her head. 'Our best chance is through the trees,' he whispered, and again her head dipped in agreement.

He glanced round and then found her hand. 'We must run,' he told her quietly. 'Ready? Come on.'

They crossed the clearing without incident and were at once hidden by the trees.

He tried to work towards the pass by climbing the rising

ground at an angle. It was a nightmare progress. Every few yards he walked into a low branch or stumbled into a bush whose thin branches whipped about with a sound like the roar of a breaking wave or so he thought. Nevertheless he felt better than he had while cooped up in the house; at times there he had felt his old claustrophobia coming on and demanding attention. This suited him much better though a glimmer of the fast waning light would be welcome. After the first troublesome fifty yards he advanced more slowly, cautiously. He held Wakhia's hand in his left as he led her on and had the dead man's automatic in his right hand.

The village behind them remained silent. By now, he reckoned, the disciples must be expecting to hear the shots which would tell them that they could go to the villagers and tell them that evil presences had been finally removed and from now on everything would be simply splendid. He guessed Nicholas longed to tell the villagers that Turikrun would become a genuine Shangri-la. Soon now, disciples would be on their way to find out what had happened.

They climbed on at a slower pace.

They had gone some distance and had just crossed a small clearing when he heard voices on ground above them. The woman heard it too. They stopped instantly. In these conditions it was impossible for him to gauge the distance between the men and themselves. The sounds of the voices slid off and round and among scores of trees.

After some seconds he led them on at an even slower pace towards the point where he reckoned the voices might have come from. Sooner or later he had either to confront them or somehow sidle past them; the latter seemed beyond possibility. Also sooner or later he had to find out if his companion had the strength for their flight and how to ensure she kept it. Women were funny creatures; they could give in for absolutely no physical reason and they could carry on without a murmur far beyond the point which quite a number of men found their limit of endurance. More and more, he tended to trust in her.

The voices became clearer as they climbed on among the trees. Between some bushes he saw lights flickering. Within another eight or ten minutes the lights became recognisable; one was from a small fire on which the men were brewing some hot drink, the other from a flashlight as one man wandered around searching for something. Halted again, listening intently, he imagined there were four of them. Others might be close or nearby but he imagined there were four distinct voices. One, deep, miserable, was given to short sentences. One was light and fluttery as a canary and had a lisp. One talked straight through whatever others were saying in a flat monotone; it sounded like a record-player or a radio announcer prattling on and on. The fourth said nothing but gave sharp barking laughs. The men spoke in a mish-mash of East European languages dominated by German, Hamburg German at that. While two argued over the precise Leninist interpretation of something written by Karl Marx – he was pretty old hat, believing that either was anything other than a useful placard for the Kremlin mob – the record-player voice gave an appreciative inventory of the qualities of a Stettin girl with buttocks hard as footballs. He fell into contemplation of lost joys.

Silk wheeled abruptly and clapped a hand over the woman's mouth as she coughed breathlessly. He held his own breath to hear if the men stopped breathing. They went straight on without interruption. When he took his hand from the woman's face she rested her forehead on his chest and hung on to him while she fought to regain normal breathing. It was some precious minutes before her fingers tightened twice on his arms as if to signal she was ready to go on.

He took the added risk of going on at a slower pace to give her time to recover. Unless he was mistaken the men were either at the top of the pass or not far from it. The light of the fire was near enough for him to see the silhouettes of most trees, blurred but nonetheless a guide. In his mind's eye he could remember the moment two evenings ago when he stood at the head of the pass and saw the hills rising on either side to the mountains beyond and the valley with its houses spread out before him in the late sunshine. After that moment and the additional eternity which had ground past since they left her house it felt unbelievable.

The illusion ended abruptly as they heard two pistol shots down in the village.

They stopped. The woman came close, seeking contact for reassurance. He could have used a bit himself.

He led her over to the nearest tree. They halted there, turning to look back down the hill. Here they were above the tops of trees lower down but the foliage of those between, combined with the still moonless sky, prevented them from seeing the village. What they did manage to glimpse were tiny gleams of light darting about, some a naked core, other a pale glow; the search of flashlights probing the darkness. That told him.

The hunt was on. Someone had found the house empty or had discovered the body of the man sent to kill them. The disciples were in a flap.

Incredibly the men up here had not yet realised that something was wrong in the village. They were talking too busily about their lost trivialities to hear the shots or heed the lights if they could see them. They were not the first guards, nor were they likely to be the last, who imagined all would be well until their relief took over.

It did not last.

But it ended strangely to his ears.

Somewhere down in the village someone loosed a fusillade of bullets. A woman's high scream came flicking to them. A man's shout ended as a gun barked. More shots came from another part of the village, marked by the intervening buildings. More people began to shout and scream.

Silence came abruptly.

Complete silence. Eerie, uncanny, out of pattern. Up here the guards had finally forgotten their diversions at home. Silk guessed they were considering four alternatives. The prisoners, the woman and himself, had escaped. Some villagers had quarrelled among themselves and involved guards. Disciples or guards had fallen out over their women. A group of the genuine drop-outs had turned on Nicholas's community. There was a fifth possibility. The villagers had rebelled and been quelled.

Silk thought it unlikely that Wakhia and he would ever know.

Events proved him wrong.

Down in the village there was another, more prolonged burst of screams and yells broken by a steely chatter of automatic rifles. A house started to burn. Its flames soared up into the darkness.

The villagers had gone into revolt in order to preserve their right to live or die according to their own way and, or so it seemed, some of the Europeans had gone over to help them.

Silk turned to the woman. 'Stay close behind me,' he warned.

They went on through the trees at a faster pace. Light from the fire and a prowling flashlight helped them now. He abandoned the caution he had employed earlier, knowing the men were listening to the commotion below and wanting to catch them unprepared.

Within minutes the woman and he reached a point where he could see the men clearly in the wavering firelight. His estimate had been wrong. There were five of them. The fifth lay sublimely asleep on the ground, head cosy on a tree-trunk, not caring a damn for anything. Deplorably from the humane point of view, they were sitting ducks.

Silk turned and made Wakhia lie down behind a tree, head towards the group of men, and then took cover behind the third tree from where she lay. He eased off the safety-catch on the automatic and took careful aim at a burning strip of branch and fired while firing and shouting went on in the village. A cloud of sparks flew over the men. They yelled alarm. The sleeper awoke, jerked to his feet, hauling out his automatic.

Inside of seconds three of them were emptying their automatics wildly into the wood. Somebody really should have warned them not to waste the stuff at night. The other two, including the erstwhile sleeper, were meeting up with old friends who had passed to another sphere.

That narrowed the odds. The other three took a sudden interest in prudence. They bellyflopped onto the ground and paused long enough to get a rough idea of where the shooting came from. Bullets whistled round him like a swarm of bees. Many whipped into the tree or those behind him. The man on the left reached the end of his clip and had to begin to roll to where he had a refill, a motion which caused him to bend his arm and raise the hand holding the automatic. One second he held it. The next he howled annoyance at the loss of more than the automatic.

Silk felt encouraged. His frequent practice stood him in good stead. Abruptly he sucked air between his teeth as a scalding sting whipped across his left upper arm and he felt blood ooze down to the elbow and stick the holed clothes to his skin. His mind was informed of some degree of pain.

One of the remaining guards also ran out of ammunition. Evidently he had a high regard for his invulnerability. He got to his feet to turn to where he could renew his ammunition but fell back alongside the fire clutching at his right shoulder.

That ended the immediate opposition temporarily. Silk knew it even before the fourth man commenced to wriggle back from the firelight into the darkness on the other side, no doubt to await help. Quickly Silk ran to Wakhia, stooping low, felt her grasp his hand, poise to raise herself, and then they turned away into the wooded darkness. Within minutes his feet felt the *hadur*, the downward slope of the pass. Within minutes they were running freely. Only the sound of their own breathing and the slap of his soles on the ground came to them.

Some time passed before he allowed them to slacken pace. This was the vital time to put as much distance between themselves and their pursuers as possible; that was a cliché but it was true, unquestionably right. He got tired of talking to himself. The woman running alongside him had achieved a remarkable degree of basic communication in the last two days, due to her intelligence and Bell's tuition rather than to his own sparkling brilliance, but on many fundamentals he had needed to be his own Watson and that was excessively tiresome. It had not improved his memory one jot.

He slowed to a stop and had to use up valuable energy to prevent Wakhia from shooting ahead like a Derby winner. No one had a right to such superb energy and stamina, he thought sourly. When he added the kindly advice to breath more easily she added insult to injury by doing it far better than he could.

The late evening air brought no sound of voices or activity from the pass. A glance behind showed him the orange brightness of the fire at the head of it. No flashlights searched yet. Temporarily some emergency in the village had prevented Nicholas and Ferdy and Hawks from sending men up there. Perhaps the noise and confusion down among the houses had prevented them from hearing the shooting going on overhead.

'We'd better get along,' he told her.

Twenty minutes later the moon shot up above the hills like an explosion. It really did look better than the poor old litter dump it had become, the trickiest bullseye in the business. His usual contempt of it turned to something near to hatred. He watched it flood this valley with its golden-yellow radiance, saw her face as clearly as if someone had lit up the sky with a sort of electricity. As she looked at him he understood why women loved the thing up there, even those who had no cause to fear daylight. She had no problem in any light.

They went on. Within minutes he stopped in his tracks. Behind them above the pass the sky held the foul clatter of a helicopter.

'Damn!' he said furiously. 'I forgot all about it. Damn damn damn!'

One glance confirmed his worst fears. The thing had a powerful light fastened to its belly which shed a light like a spotlight over the ground beneath it. It circled around as if probing the wood they had left.

It did not stay there long. Within a few minutes it came sailing up the track towards them. The wood ahead seemed a hell of a way off.

15

They were given no chance to relax. Hour after hour the helicopter clattered near them, its light scanning the ground like a baleful eye, hovering if those inside thought they detected any sliver of shadow worthy of closer attention. On one occasion when it hung motionless against moonlight smeared like butter over the sky its light turned around searching the ground with the intensity of one of those joyless multimillionaire recluses searching the floor for a dropped ha'penny. That suggested the chopper contained at least three people: the pilot, someone who operated the light on its circular axis, and a third individual who, with the pilot, could study the ground while the light was manipulated. In this terrain the gadget had great value. Twice the machine floated directly above them like a boat riding at its moorings. Each time he felt convinced the light would penetrate the well-leafed canopy of branches overhead and pinpoint them where they crouched against two adjacent trees. Each time his fears proved unfounded. The thing lifted away and clattered off to scan another area. He did not uncross his fingers. What went away could come back. And another problem was already developing.

Within a short time of the woman and himself reaching the wood he had counted more than twenty men equipped with flashlights infiltrating into the valley and spreading out across it in a line like beaters intending to flush them out. He guessed that there were as many men without flashlights or holding them in abeyance to save batteries as those holding the probing lights. Although the men were some distance off and forced to advance slowly on account of the darkness he took no joy from what could only be a temporary advantage. In fact he felt inhibited. What with the thing grinding away above, the men coming on, the darkness here among the trees as he and the woman went on so that it proved increasingly awkward to leap nimbly forward without risking breaking one or both legs or knocking yourself out cold on a malevolent tree, he saw no reason to cheer. Somehow they managed to move on though at a slower pace than the men hunting them.

At one point his usually saintly disposition deserted him. The silence of his companion irritated him. He knew it unfair, inexcusably unworthy; it wasn't her fault, God help her, that an accident of life had denied her speech. But for a few lonely moments he had a sharp desire to exchange words with some-one about any damn daft thing, the weather, which theatrical genius was playing the zoo game of switching mates for a week or so, the value of Picasso's later work in 2000 A.D. when most people except the twittery art experts would know it was not art, any old trivia which made bombshell headlines of importance which created a furore for Friday back home. He needed to lessen the tensions which had not slackened much since he first peered down the holes in his mind.

As the chopper prowled back towards them he pulled the woman up against a tree and put a hand on the back of her neck to keep her head lowered and prevent her from gazing up as she had one earlier occasions when it came near them. This time the thing clattered straight on to examine the nearest hump of hillside on their left, lurching away in its threatening fashion. In a weak moment he hauled the woman close and fussed her mouth and used his hands to let her know he liked the woman-shape she was and because, well, he couldn't commit himself to words about the unfairness which had been in his mind. Naturally she had not the vaguest notion what caused his sudden capriciousness. But being a nice healthy soul she let her response imply that precisely the same thought had been on her mind for a long time. He felt even more contrite.

'Don't worry,' he told her. 'Directly we get away from here I'll make sure you're taken care of properly. Our friend Bell put you in my care and I'll look after you. We'll take you away from here and see if anything can be done about your voice and get you educated. If you want those things. So try not to worry.'

She kissed him as if he was an archangel.

Behind them the voices of their pursuers suddenly sounded alarmingly near. They always did after the old banger din of the helicopter faded and he could distinguish other sounds more clearly again. This time he could tell the men were nearer. Some of them must have worked ahead of the main line.

He pulled her on again. They ran round a pool of moonlight into another narrow shadow-blackened strip towards a broad chalk-white stretch of direct radiance full of the heavy sweetish scent of night-flowering bushes, and on into a long dim tunnel where every positive shape was only a bare half-shade darker than the gloom around it. He longed to be out in the light. But there they would have no cover. And here their feet made scarcely any sound. And for once nature was on his side. They had not disturbed any of the night-birds and marmots he had expected them to put up with their various notes of betrayal.

Behind them men started to shoot at shadows. Voices shouted urgently. Both were overlaid by the whining rattle of the returning helicopter.

Shortly before midnight they had slowed to a gentler pace. Although uncomplaining, the woman was tired, her feet stumbling, her hand holding his tighter. He was not surprised. They had been walking or running under constant pressure for hours now with scarcely any pauses for genuine rest. The last hour had brought its own problem as they had to walk over several belts of stones which did not do her naked feet any good. It was the stones which let him know that the elasticity was going from his own legs. No doubt it would return if necessity demanded but it would help if they could rest for a while.

Behind and above them the night had quietened somewhat. Nicholas and his associates underestimated her resolution and his determination. The helicopter had headed back to the village some time ago, no doubt to refuel and find out if they had been discovered or sighted somewhere there. As he looked back now the flashlights were farther away, down to the gleam of cat's-eyes except for two over on the left where the valley floor started to rise. Such temporary advantages gave him no consolation. Until dawn the walking men could follow at the same methodical pace unless they found some sign which caused them to hurry. The beaters had no reason to hurry, only to be thorough. And at first light the helicopter would return to search the whole area in more favourable conditions and to pick up and drop men to search any suspect area where Wakhia and he might be hiding.

Abruptly he stopped, so abruptly that she went on for several paces until her own tired mind told her that he was no longer beside her. She turned wearily, looking at him through the moonlight. I must have been going out of my mind even worse than I thought, he told himself as he searched carefully along the waistband of his trousers on either side. Only a few seconds proved that he had indeed forgotten something else. Carefully he turned back the material on the right side and fidgeted with a tiny plastic zip concealed in a fold between the trouser material and the lining; from the little pocket the zip had held fast he fingered out two wakey-wakey pills in their soluble glassine covers. His infernal memory had forgotten them; perhaps that was just as well for he would have been tempted to use them earlier, but he should have remembered they were there.

He padded on to join Wakhia and showed her what he held

in his hand. Briefly he told her what they were for and how they should both take one now in order to stay awake. Moonlight flecked her eyes as she raised her partly shadowed head to look at his face. He closed his hand over the pills and shook them and opened his hand and picked one up and swallowed it.

'You don't have to feel frightened,' he told her. 'They don't do any harm.'

Reassured, she did what he had said. He saw her grimace as she swallowed the pill. 'Just wait for a moment,' he told her.

When they went on he carried the basket containing their food and the extra ammunition. They had done it in turns ever since they reached the foot of the climb to the pass. Gradually they went on more strongly, the pills lessening their sense of mental fatigue and seeming to put new strength into their legs. He put his hand on her arm and asked if she knew of a cave farther on where they could rest, say, in about an hour, some cave where there were many caves and higher up. For several minutes she did not answer. Then she took his hand with a positiveness that was a reply in itself.

Farther back down the valley men began to shoot again. He glanced back and saw they were farther away. The shots must be attributable to guile, an attempt to flush the hunted to betray themselves by a rush. If the flashlights were true, the men were searching one of the woods in which she and he had sheltered over an hour ago. The trees partly muffled the sound of firing. After some moments it died away into a few desultory shots.

They walked on through the silence under the wheeling stars for over an hour until she changed direction abruptly and led them up a slope thick with rocks and boulders until they came to the sixth or seventh of circular black openings with more on either side and several more above. He assumed that they must have some connection underground with perhaps another outlet elsewhere as such caves often did. It was a good thing she had spent her youth becoming acquainted with the shape and pecularities of these hills.

She led him down into darkness.

When daylight came he was sitting at the entrance listening to the rattle of the helicopter coming nearer and nearer. For some hours Wakhia had been resting, not asleep he guessed, but lying quiet some distance inside the entrance. Twice since they reached here they had walked a short distance to where she knew of a tiny stream of water trickling down the hillside. On those occasions the whole world around them seemed peaceful. Nothing had stirred. Nothing had grated. The moon had fallen, leaving the sky to the fading stars.

He saw sunlight glint on the distant nose of the chopper and decided it best to remain where they were rather than be panicked into flight. Even if they escaped detection, some flurry of falling stones disturbed by their feet might attract attention by a man with binoculars. He also wanted to know if Nicholas and Ferdy intended to put any new strategy into operation.

Alone, he watched for over an hour while the helicopter prowled up and down the valley. It spent most of its time hovering over strips of woodland like a bee investigating a flower, and it crawled along over paths on the curved hillside opposite like someone in a bathchair. Later he saw a file of men creep along one of the higher paths almost directly opposite and near where the helicopter seemed to sway at anchor; then they went charging down the hill and plunged into the wood. Within half-an-hour the men re-emerged on the Turikrun side of the trees and the chopper landed near them. Two of the men held a brief consultation with someone inside the machine. Directly it ended the chopper swung up into the air and turned towards Turikrun. The men followed it.

Watching them go, slowly, tiredly, worn by their long walk through the heat and disappointment after a sleepless night, he became conscious of Wakhia kneeling beside him. She had obviously seen what happened. Her eyes asked a question and she looked up the valley in the opposite direction to that taken by the men. He shook his head; he did not think it wise to go on now. A brief nod was followed by an instruction by her hands and eyes that he should have a rest while she kept guard. Perhaps it was foolish to agree but he did so without question. He stood up, thumping his head on the roof of the cave and crept cautiously down into the darkness, rubbing the place he had bumped.

He awoke abruptly to find Wakhia kneeling beside him. Automatically he cursed himself for taking such a risk and looked at his watch. It was getting on for four o'clock in the afternoon. He had been asleep for hours.

'You should have woken me up,' he chided.

For another moment he indulged the luxury of lying still to collect his wits. The fingers-and-toes routine proved that his brain still controlled them without trouble. Yawning he sat up and stretched his arms. His mouth tasted normal. On impulse he gave her a polite acknowledgement of gratitude for letting him sleep.

They got up cautiously and went outside for a breath of fresh air and dived back into the cave immediately.

Away in the distance the helicopter was coming up the valley towards them. Although it was some distance off they saw it clearly, which meant its occupants could have seen them if they were looking in this direction. Inside the entrance he pulled her alongside him so that they stood with their backs to the wall on the side from which the chopper was approaching. Just in time his still sleep-plagued mind realised that the tin gnat could hover just off the hillside and might be able to direct its light in here. He told her to lie on the floor and flopped down beside her.

The clatter increased until the din seemed to set the whole

cave vibrating around them. Suddenly it had almost reached them. It was a pretty damn daft thing to do but he held his breath as if the men could hear him. For several minutes they were deafened and the cave shuddered like a bride's first jelly. Then the noise gradually died. As it faded he got up shaking his head and helped her to rise, a courtesy which seemed to embarrass her.

She looked a query at him and he shook his head. 'It will come back,' he said. 'It's bound to come back because they don't want us to escape.' She nodded.

Nearly an hour later they were sitting just inside the entrance of the cave eating some of the fruit she had brought for their journey when the helicopter reappeared going down the valley about two-thirds of the way up the opposite hillside. It droned straight ahead at an unhurried pace without any sign that it intended to detour. That struck him as more than strange. It might be taking someone back to the valley or returning from an appointment elsewhere. Strange. He frowned as it dwindled to a speck which vanished from sight against a slab of sunlit hilltip. Nicholas or Ferdy was up to something.

The rush of theories going through his head was interrupted by the clutch of Wakhia's hand. He saw she had turned towards him, her face full of excitement, like a child. Her free hand pointed down the hillside to the floor of the valley and she pretended to pant. Her eyes pleaded.

'Very well,' he agreed, full of misgiving. 'I need a drink myself. And I'd like a wash.'

She smiled and showed how the dust in the cave had covered her hands and clogged her nails.

Methodically they prepared to resume their journey. He became the prey of anxieties of detail which he had managed to ignore until now. This was always the worst period, the last stretch of a journey.

While he examined the revolver and automatic to ensure they worked he adjusted himself to a belief that they might not be able to reach Chitral for two more days at least, perhaps three or four. There was reason. How long it had taken him to regain consciousness after whatever caused him to lose his memory he did not know with any degree of reliability. Nor did he know how far he had been from Chitral when that event happened. He had a feeling, no more, that it had been only a short journey. The belief simply hung in his mind like one of those things you cannot recall instantly though it always seems about to come back.

The automatic had only three bullets left. Thereafter it would be useless. That shortened their chances. The revolver would be their only line of defence. When it ran out of ammunition they could either be killed or hauled back to Turikrun by Nicholas's disciples. He would have preferred to face that situation alone.

As he finished his tasks he saw Wakhia watching him. Her own preparations were complete. He hoped he was not becoming to impressible about bright eyes and warm remembered body. Men could be monstrously naive.

He smiled, too damn cheerfully. 'Right,' he said. 'I'm ready.'

This time she helped him to stand, as if he were peculiarly precious.

He glanced round to be sure they had left nothing which would tell any disciple they had halted here. It seemed clean. 'Come on,' he said.

They had walked a mile or so along a track worn by goats and other animals on this long rounded hillside when they came in sight of a wide stretch of woodland on the valley floor. At one moment a thought crossed his mind and he asked if the man they saw shot dead on the hillside the evening he had arrived was Bell, and she nodded and turned her head aside. Later a hand on his arm stopped him and she pointed down; she touched his chest and then her own and pointed at the wood again. He saw a shy sort of smile on her lips. The smile explained her meaning.

'Gracious! was it?' he queried. 'Was that where we met?'

She nodded. Her smile deepened. For some extraordinary reason she seemed jolly pleased with herself. And perhaps she should be, having recognised him from the description given her by Bell.

He took another look around. In this particular instant they might well be the last two survivors of a planet devastated by some man-made holocaust. The hillsides were barren with here and there spills of talus large or small, a litter of boulders like dinosaurs eggs sprinkled around. Those who had grown up here or known it from childhood must have learned to tell their distance from or to a place by whichever sprinkle of boulders they had reached.

He saw no other living creature. Not even a bird. They could indeed be 'on the beach,' the two doomed to start the whole damn business again, a shuddersome responsibility. He looked up the valley to a small clump of woodland and back along the patched bare earth with its strips of tough old grass and centenarian bush to the larger wood almost below them.

A glance at the sky told him it would not begin to pale for at least two hours. He did not relish their being out in the open for that length of time. Once seen, they would have scant chance of survival.

While the world around them maintained its flat empty stillness of earth tortured long ago he led the way down from one pile of boulders to the next. At least they had the advantage of being no more significant in such a landscape than two ants.

At the edge of the wood, while the woman went ahead through the trees, he paused to glance up at the hills and instantly his stomach went tight.

16

He did not like it one bit.

High up on either side of the valley were patrols of men. They were walking slowly towards Turikrun along what appeared to be from this angle the rim of each hillside, their figures outlined against the cloudless sky. From what he could see, there were at least fourteen men in each patrol. For a moment he wondered how on earth they could have got there from the village; he had an impression that each patrol had come to this point where he could see them from some distance closer to Chitral; their numbers meant that the helicopter, if only one was involved, must have taken several journeys to drop so many men at their starting point; how on earth could he have been unaware of them? Gradually it dawned on his dim wits that the chopper must have flown over while he lay asleep in the cave and the woman had assumed it was merely hunting for sight of them and had decided against rousing him, her female logic telling her that if the thing merely flew back and forth without stopping it must be all right and she need not try to tell him about it. Fair enough, he would have done the same.

All of the men appeared to have chest and back malformations. That meant they were carrying an oldfashioned type of field walkie-talkie set which kept them individually in touch with those opposite and probably with the helicopter; they had automatic rifles slung over their shoulders. He hoped that

Nicholas had been unable to spare another patrol of equal or even lesser size to come down the valley. That could well end their chance of escape. He tried to cheer himself up with a thought that if the villagers had indeed revolted last evening it would be impossible for Nicholas to leave the village lightly defended today; both Nicholas and Ferdy knew they had to salvage whatever they could from the wreck of a carefully prepared scheme, if only to save their own necks from their rulers' fury. The size of the patrols up there suggested they were positioned to have the widest view possible, thereby to save men for other duties. It also suggested that Nicholas and Ferdy were army officers used to such operations elsewhere.

He found he was no longer alone. Silently the woman had returned to join him and stood watching the patrols high up as they paced methodically forward. Her lips showed a slight constriction. His stomach still felt like a sheet being wrung out. Twentyeight men was an awful lot of men, with weapons and a gadget which could bring reinforcements droning through the sky.

They stood watching as the men walked slowly on along the crest of the hills pausing only to gaze down into the valley and then go on again.

He let some moments pass until he had cause to believe that neither the woman nor he had been seen. She stood bleak as an official statue, eyes huge in her stiff face. Unsure if he was doing the right thing he turned her round and pointed ahead. They ran through the wood and halted at the other end, just inside the trees at a point from where they had a clear view up the valley and of the hillcrests. The scene appeared to be deserted. Nothing caught his attention. No sound of voices came to him. Once again they could have been the sole survivors on the beach. His stomach distrusted the stillness, the bland silence, and told him that he would have to live for a long time in experience with the sheet being wrung slowly inside, dripping icy cold water into his guts. Still unsure, he turned to the woman. She shook her head, as if confirming that she neither heard nor saw anything. Belatedly a dreadful fear came to him, that she and he had already been seen and the men on the hills behind them would soon come down and join together, if they had not already done so, and come walking up the valley again, closing in on them and driving them towards another line of men advancing from the Chitral end; a nightmare thought. He yanked up a smile as reliable as a fairground balloon.

'Let's go back to that stream and have a wash,' he said. Very quietly.

Several times after darkness spread overhead they heard shooting. It was faint and came from farther down the valley. Once it was unmistakably automatic fire. On other occasions he recognised single fire shots, either one or several separated by seconds. He paid careful attention to each burst as he lay quiet on the grass. Some yards away Wakhia was restless, as wide-awake as himself, but more plagued by inability to relax. Occasionally she sighed and turned on her side and then turned onto her back again.

No longing for sleep bothered him. He was far too busy fretting over whether he had done right in deciding they should stay here or whether it would not have been better to go on, protected by various forms of darkness which would soon be gone. He knew that; they lay between the stream and a wide circular patch of pale moonlight and each time he glanced at the patch he saw that its shape and emphasis had changed as the moon shifted over into another vault of sky and caused some benighted traveller to wonder if he was going to arrive in the right place on time and offer a prayer to save all politicians from the perils of life and human nature on the bit of grit they left behind.

Some time later his homilies and deep important thoughts, the sort of things professional agents thought about during hours of stress in order to spare themselves from the dangers of overthinking about their immediate problem, were interrupted by knowledge of a not unpleasant warmth nearer to him than it should have been. She was a very tense woman, content that he should understand how tense from her utter stillness. His mild attempt to get her to relax did not succeed. That was understandable. She knew the old life of her village had gone, that it had joined those in other valleys here which the modern age had killed with progress, and that she was adrift, between the lost familiar and the unfound unknown. And with her disability and lack of skills for what the unknown might demand of her. It was understandable. A good many women back in the lands of triumphant progress found it all a bit much, and they had been born into the rumpus and weaned on its juices. He understood her fears.

He took her hand and said: 'Don't worry. I know you think it's going to be awkward and strange, but you'll get alone fine. I'll come whenever I can, to straighten out any problems and the people who will help you will be the best people. So try not to worry. It'll be all right.'

Her lips sought his with the fierceness of those who wanted to know they had kissed before dying.

Soon after dawn they halved their remaining supply of goats' cheese and fruit and bread and halved it again to give them a scratch meal now with one last share for the remainder of their journey, however long that might be.

He knew that by this time tomorrow they would be damned hungry and near a point when they would have to risk going at a faster pace even if it meant they expended more energy. True, they might face worse problems but it was no earthly use twittering about them now. Fortunately she was quieter. His thoughts swung off at a tangent. It occurred to him that he probably understood her better because no fog of words prevented genuine communication between them on essentials.

186

When they finished their meal they went to the stream to wash again. An overnight warmth still lingered among the trees and no coldness struck as he stripped off his shirt and knelt down to wash staleness off his chest and shoulders. Wakhia finished quicker than he did and he was aware of her rising to her feet. As he sluiced the back of his neck he heard a rasp in her throat and then another, higher, a positive note, and he suddenly heard her screaming like an ordinary woman, her throat full of terror. Startled, he glanced round and saw where she was looking. He fell, still kneeling, flinging himself forward on the ground, his feet dangling in the stream. There was nothing else he could do.

Although the man who had been pacing warily towards them through the trees must be a hundred yards off his face was momentarily clear as he sprang through a shaft of sunlight and dived for cover. In the instant of recognition the morning took on a nightmare unreality. Silk felt violently sick. The world swung and bucketed around him. For a few horrible seconds he thought he might be on the verge of insanity or about to pass out in a faint. Without warning, the holes in his mind filled as he recognised the man and seemed to spill over with memory for the man was Angus Wallace, the little friend in Rawalpindi, the double agent with the Rus wife, and it was all new and unexpected and his mind screamed for time to work out the complications. He had no time. They were being shot at from behind the tree. His shouts to the woman went unheeded. She seemed content to simply stand there indulging a luxury of unbelievable sound with almost voluptuous insanity, wholly regardless of danger, pausing only to draw sufficient breath to scream again if hypnotised by what she heard coming from her own throat. The noise went on and on as he picked up the revolver which had lain beside him and rolled over and over as rapidly as he could until he reached her and coiled his arm round her legs. The scream went on as she fell; he was sure every nook and surface up in the hills around them heard it and threw it back down the valley to a score of waiting men. As she hit the ground she started to cry.

It did not take genius to realise that something had unnerved their assailant. He kept shooting wild. Bullets gnatted around, ricocheted off tree-trunks, plunged into the ground. None came anywhere near. Either the long eerie scream had unnerved him, or, more likely, he had wrenched a muscle in his gun arm as he hit the ground and had lost control of his hand. That was a sort of revenge. Silk overcame a rush of impulses to remember and think and managed somehow to know he must end the shooting quickly or the whole valley might fill up with disciples and guards. It might be too late already. Two more shots reverberated among the trees, the bullets flicking up through branches and foliage overhead. In the silence which followed a confetti of leaf fragments floated down to settle on the ground.

He stayed quiet. Events had happened too swiftly for him to accept any immediate plan; he could still feel cold water trickling out of his hair down the back of his neck. Wakhia was still crying, body heaving, mouth pressed to the grass, hands clawing at the ground. He kept whispering to her to keep quiet but she was gone too far on a journey of her own, a new knowledge about herself, to heed him. So he had to risk it. He started to edge forward to the nearest tree likely to afford some cover. Once he looked round and found her following him although she was still crying.

It took him several minutes of going from tree to tree to come within sight of the other man again. He saw no sign of movement, the body limp, the head twisted at a very strange angle. Unconvinced, he told the woman to stay here and spared an extra moment to ask if she understood and heard her whisper an astonished yes and then yesyesyesyes yes yes yesyesyes in a raw husky accent but gaining confidence. She was whispering as he walked forward. He could only imagine what she felt like in these moments; he knew his own debt to her attempt to save him. He knelt down beside the man; and saw that in one of those freak accidents which do happen the man had miscalculated as he jumped, and struck the side of his head on the tree at an awkward angle as he went down and the collision broke his neck. The shooting had been caused by muscular contraction. Silk felt cheated.

As slowly as he dared he searched the dead man's clothes. All the while he listened to the dawn and the whispering voice. His search failed to discover anything of interest. Yet he guessed that either Nicholas or Ferdy had stepped out of line to contact him and order him to come into the valley from this end to help men who had been ordered to go back to the village. He had nearly completed his search when the woman screamed again.

A voice called as he grabbed the revolver. '*C'est moi.*' He recognised it. Murmur emerged from behind a tree. '*Bonjour m'sieu, 'moiselle.*'

'And a frantically happy Common Market to you. What brought you?'

'A funny yarn. So I followed. You all right?'

'Hungry,' Silk said and stood up. He had not the faintest intention of telling anyone what happened to his memory during his debriefing; that would lose him his job, people being so damned fussy these days. 'You look pretty in that hat. Where did you get it?'

'At a riot during a cricket match. People feel things so deeply, man. Bowl for the head, boy, bowl for the head. You have a pretty friend.'

'That's quite a story. If it wasn't for her I'd be dead. I inherited her.'

'What could be nicer,' Murmur commented, 'even for a dead man.' The story he told contained no surprises in its account of how the porters tried to kill both of them for what they carried and how the teller of the tale escaped to tell of his anguish at the tragic end of one of his dearest friends. Yesterday an

189

unknown man contacted him at the hotel and he drove off;
Murmur had followed him to a rendezvous with a man who
arrived by helicopter. That suggested contact was gained by a
transmitter in the helicopter. The rest of it fell into position.

'Ah,' Silk said, and nodded. 'Well, let's get started. I've a
good deal to tell you.'

They were near the main road. Nothing had happened.
Everything was quiet. That was all. For now. Tomorrow . . .
although the government should help the valley people get rid
of the plague of gurus the Turikrunis would soon find this age
hounding them in other forms, many would disappear, another
wild corner would be lost and taken over by a rush of medi-
ocrity arriving with plastic faces in plastic cars, with plastic
food wrapped in plastic containers . . . try a package holiday in
the hills of Pakistan and the fabulous Khyber Pass, folks, where
Kipling found immortal poetry and Corporal Jones died as he
picked nits out of his hair, see the historic places where the
Army of the Indus was slaughtered with its wives and children
by the Afghans, come on, folk, the adventure of a lifetime for
only . . . yach!

'You're uncommon silent,' Murmur commented. 'Twenty
minutes and not a word. Are you sickening?'

'Huh!' Silk said sourly. 'No, my tongue is salivating, getting
ready to shovel. What goodies have we up here? Iced melon
soaked in white wine? Shrimp soup with lemon juice? Smoked
Scotch salmon? Whole bullock roasted on the spit? Plump
Norfolk turkey, preferably cold? Banana flambeau saturated in
brandy? Devon cream and iced raspberries? Stilton with a tang
of port in every crumb? Van der Humm? By golly, I'm doing
myself a mischief just thinking about it!'